VAGABOND
Chic

Solitude, Hot Flashes, Other Exhilarations

Presented To
Plympton Public Library

Given By
Helen Reynolds
(sister of the author!)

GLORIA JEAN

PAGE PUBLISHING, INC.
New York, NY

First originally published by Page Publishing, Inc. 2016

ISBN 978-1-68348-078-5 (pbk)
ISBN 978-1-68348-079-2 (digital)

Printed in the United States of America

For my daughter, my angel and navigator
Michele Linn
January 1969—April 2013

In loving memory

It's not Mt. Everest. It's a drive in a freakin' car!

In 1960 John Steinbeck, age fifty-eight, bought a pickup truck, placed a camper on top, and left his home on Long Island for a drive around America with his poodle companion—I was a twenty something when the charm of *Travels with Charley* first struck. Looking back on it, the idea of taking my own solitary jaunt came about through a window of circumstance, as most brainstorms do. And in my condition—you know, middle age, life being so short and all, wedged at a crossroad, knocked back at the time by personal loss— my deadened soul experienced a timely draft. With little in mind but some stale imagination and no thought of what might be done with the rest of my life, there it came, another reminder of Mr. Steinbeck's vagrancy, his spell a persistent reach from the cosmos: *Get up, Gloria Jean, here's what wants to happen.* Something took hold. It was out of my hands.

Aside from certain freedoms bestowed on middle age, it may have been a trip to Florida two years earlier that inspired the journey, or at least a vigorous nudge to that end. Was the idea of navigating alone beyond New England so unthinkable for a *woman my age?* The vision continued to unfold like leaves in random swirls across the yard, a compelling, relentless collaboration with fate: that at the end of those days and miles in outer space there would be something to write from another street. Weathers would be weathered, loneliness endured, and scenes photographed. Small town, back-road America would be browsed. So at age fifty-five, I departed New Hampshire and headed west, sans poodle, in a flashy *Geo Prizm* the color of taupe.

> "…we do not take a trip; a trip takes us. Tour masters, schedules, reservations brass-bound and inevitable, dash themselves to wreckage on the personality of the trip. Only when this is recognized can the blown-in-the-glass bum relax and go along with it. Only then do the frustrations fall away. In this, a journey is like marriage. The certain way to be wrong is to think you control it. I feel better now having said this, although only those who have experienced it will understand it."
>
> —John Steinbeck
> *Travels with Charley: In Search of America*

CHAPTER 1

Heart of Hotness—
The humidity! The humidity!

October 1992. South Florida's dawn whispered its farewell in breathtaking Disney fashion with an endless chorus line of palm trees fringing the interstate as small flocks of birds seemed to burst on cue from the mist in random silhouette. And did I mention the glowing violet backdrop?

Decompression was setting in as I headed for West Palm Airport and a return flight to New England's frosty hills, far from the steamy venue of Wendy's wedding. Its imagery filtered through my brain in a wonderful dream I struggled to preserve—the rugged Spanish beauty of the stone church with its towering stained glass images, candles gripped in wrought iron spires at the end of each pew, ushers lighting them along the aisle with quiet grace. The bride, in her Victorian gown and silk-high button boots, echoed her teen portrayal of Emily in *Our Town,* now in her own *real* wedding. My mind replayed the reception over and over, of Wendy dancing with her father in dream-like swirls to a country tune he sang to her as a child, a moment most tender, her macho trucker dad, jaws tightly clenched, holding a concentrated grip—stifling.

This was my first trip alone, not as a tourist, but time with friends who had migrated south years before—time with the neighbors, southerners speaking in drawl, a polite rhythm I'd nearly forgotten from grade school in Rhode Island, the navy base and its steady influx of temporary school pals out of Pensacola.

Back at the house, a few couples straggled in for a nightcap after the reception. One of them I had met earlier; in another time and place he could be Jimmy Smits as Rhett Butler. "Ah'm from kis-sIMee," he drawled. *Frankly,* I wished he could drawl a few pages aloud, or at least a couple of sentences. He and a few others remained till four in the morning discussing troops in Somalia and October's annual snowbird invasion. Oh, and Florida State. My feeble contribution was affirmation of New England's weather: that, yes, people *up there* survive day to day scraping ice from windshields. One of them said he had been as far north as the Carolinas once, but it was February and as cold as he intended to get. He did point out that "the people up there are nice enough, I guess." I tried to picture any one of them in a turtleneck. It's the middle of October as they all rejoice: the weather has broken—from sauna to sweltering, my menopausal self surmised. I in turn enthused about my dip in the pool that morning, my glorious encounter with the tropics in water that plunged to seventy-five degrees.

Aside from the wedding, there was that meeting a few days earlier with an odd-looking turtle. It sported a long snout, so I called him Cyrano. His goal that morning was to swim in the chlorine pond, while the resident dog, a Chinese Chin—short on stature but a guard dog nonetheless—confronted the reptile from all possible angles, bouncing with yelping darts, mostly at Cyrano's head. At one point the annoyed turtle managed to flip in the air in protest to its canine annoyance. Each bark caused its snout to withdraw, and in the alternating silence Cyrano's head would emerge in perfect cadence as it happened with the porch radio and George Jones's exquisite wail–turtle head in: *"They placed a wreath upon his door…"* head out: *"and soon they'll carry him away…"* head in: *He stopped loving hURrr toDAYeee."* I ask you, is there any better serenade for that lonesome soul nursing his drink in a darkened lounge?

In a thank-you note to my hosts, I suggested Cyrano be moved to the savannahs a half mile down the street—chlorine-free/turtle-friendly—a similar kindness performed years earlier for *Phred,* a one-eyed *phrog* scooped repeatedly from my New Hampshire pool. Spinning the yarn of Phred's relocation, by me, by car, to a bog down on Church Road, always gets an interesting second look.

Time-Out: *The Florida soft shell turtle has a long neck and elongated head with a snorkel-like nose, dark brown to olive green, leathery carapace, and a cream-colored underside.*

Oh, ***that*** Mojo!

Meanwhile, back on the road, gracious palm trees aside, my return home had hit a snag south of West Palm, the airport I expected to reach from Exit 5, the exit I just passed, and out of absolute panic—common sense not in play here—took the next ramp, coming to a dead-end, quarter-mile of pavement that for no other reason I could see merely dissected a flat strip of land.

Snowy egrets browsed a nearby swale, plumage glistening white on white in the morning sun, all of them unconcerned with my desperate circumstance. Just when my timing was right on, time to spare. Seconds ticked by like *Final Jeopardy,* its mocking ditty pinging through my head. I'll miss the plane. I could be robbed! Travelers get robbed when they're lost. I have to catch the plane, dammit! Think! I sat frozen in Florida's heat beside a grassy knoll. Jim would have said, "Do something, even if it's wrong!" I and the egrets waited for the robbers.

So there it was. If life were a drain, mine continued its swirl to center. Jim's life had ended, and until this trip south for the wedding, I'd been replaying our six-year nightmare from the couch—trips to the hospital, the oncologist, transfusions, chemo, blood counts, six years of wait and see...what are the red counts...wait and see, today we'll try this...there are options; wait and see, inch by inch; sporadic elation flared with *relative* good news, a deceiving new  lease, our rollercoaster of torment, the outside world a distant place. Why does my mind keep going there?

Back at the swale, it occurred to me that the airport was straight across the marsh from where I sat. Two egrets broke from the group and seemed to strut with purpose across the grass, stopping nearby, tipping their heads from side to side without looking directly my way, as in a private conversation; a committee of some kind? Judging? I was nearly self-conscious. My inner child wished for talking egrets. *Look there, across the way, they nodded, planes are lifting and landing. Why not go back to Exit 5? You should probably turn around.*

My personal *mojo* was first prompted on that Florida plain, traveling alone for the first time, renting a car, reading maps, navigating the unknown, every arrival an astonishing triumph, until the exit, the missed exit. Occasional reminders in the months to follow of that *extraordinary conquest* would serve to sustain inner resolve over the long run.

Further north, Delta's flight out of Newark was delayed twenty minutes, prompting *New Yawk* grumbles from an elder seated behind: "This never happened when it was *Eastern*," she muttered to her son. And as if the memory of Florida's kiss good-bye were not enough, I seemed to be the only one, head pressed against the window for this pass over Central Park, Manhattan's spires illuminated with the brassy gold of late afternoon, and beyond that, New England's vermilion woods, the mother of all foliage tours.

CHAPTER 2

The Hathaway Connection

Wilfred Hathaway loved to drive. And he loved to travel. So it's in my genes, the Hathaway genes, my father's map-reading, drive-here-to-there-nonstop genes. A mechanic from birth, he was born on Groundhog Day 1918, wearing denim bib overalls, working much of his life in, under, and around farm machinery—potato harvesters and other such contraptions munching Rhode Island's countryside. And if there's a time in my life when Wilfred Hathaway wasn't sliding on a cart beneath something with a motor, driving it, discussing a recent drive and the best way to get there, what he was driving, what kind of engine it had, fixing it, or who he bought it *off 'n,* memory of much else is gone, but for the instant image of his garage that springs to mind with the slightest whiff of grease and motor oil. His hands wash in my memory, swirling hairy hands foaming with lather, fingers weaving, washing for supper—the unforgettable aroma of Lava soap.

He bought a truck camper in 1962, the dawn of the RV age, and thereafter we traipsed our land, *Bedouins* of Rand McNally. Holidays, weekends, summer vacations, each trek, long or short, with a different mix of family and friends, Wilfred ever at the wheel, to Maine, New Brunswick, Florida, the southwest, and from San Diego to the Alaska Highway, each day a long, long drive, concluding *hundreds of thousands* of miles later it seemed. Motto: "You went to the bathroom before we left."

He was also a collector, and across the miles my father rummaged the landscape for America's jewelry—insulators, thick domes of colored glass found mostly on telephone poles. Between Rhode Island and Alaska, he searched railroad beds, flea markets and junk shops, and after he died, I realized how many he had accumulated. Some three hundred or more were displayed on a steel lazy Susan, a multilevel pyramid the size of a small refrigerator collecting dust in his garage, and from this corner of his estate I chose an assortment of colors. They're light catchers now, windowsill legacies of porcelain, cobalt blue, carnival glass, and translucent shades of green, violet, and aquamarine. Insulators, and my search for one in the journey to come, would become a quest—one more insulator to place at my father's grave.

His heart stopped at the age of sixty-four, the father with whom I shared only occasional space in childhood—Pearl Harbor, divorce, his sister took me in and there I stayed—same town, different house, not so unusual a circumstance for those times, I suppose. Perspective changes child to adult, an older prism, the parent with a history, never really discussed or explained, gone now, things sorted, passed along, pieces kept, fragments of memory, long journeys in middle age, the search for an insulator—*mojo* before I knew what it was.

CHAPTER 3

Flashback, April 1992

How could sleep have stolen that hour? Jim's life ended "after a long illness" while I and his son dozed beside his bed. Fifty years of his life and six years of *terminal anguish* stopped; we slept. Death comes at us daily, it seems, *details at eleven*, mothers wailing for a child or a husband slain, starving faces of the third world gaze blankly into our living space, a gaunt distant agony. Desensitized, I thought, until now.

Jim's last five weeks were spent in the hospital among his comrades in Oncology. Others departed as Hospice prepared a nearby room, allowing families to gather in vigil with their loved one in the final hours. Moans are heard from that space as I leave the hospital at night, the room empty in the morning. Was that to come for us? When? Is this the end? Will it happen here?

Friends visit, trying helplessly to *be there,* while family, clinging to tenderness, fighting impatience and fatigue, wonder where strength has gone, where Jim has gone. Nurses, loving mothers who warm the room, push through a frenzied day of their own, while specialists seek language to explain that day's test or what might be done tomorrow, or after the weekend. A death watch, here in my heart, a concept that, until now was always…later.

I'm doing it again, forgetting it was he caught in the malignant web, and we, the feeble spectators. His departure began six years earlier with the bleak diagnosis: non-Hodgkins lymphoma, two to six years, the sentence that put an end to life as we knew it. He faded from himself in a subtle chemical transfer, can't remember when he left, as though a hermit crab had found its malevolent shell and stood at its door, Jim no longer there, while *"It"* remained.

Hushed conversations pass across his bed in the final week, interrupted at times by *It,* the dementia demanding to be wheeled through the halls again, or refusing food. *It* wants me to stay at night, there in *It's* bed, "…but don't get too close, don't touch my skin, too heavy, painful…wait! Don't leave the room…I'm afraid to go to sleep…they're out there doing something…I've heard them talking…please don't go home…stay…sleep…I'll watch for them. More pain meds…did you write it down? We must keep track… they aren't paying attention…you must write everything down…and the time, don't forget the time…just took Prednisone…this damn machine is out…need more morphine…No! Don't call the nurses… they're mad at me…where's my doctor?"

He bolts from the bed to avoid "dust falling from the ceiling… the room is going to cave in…" His jaw is clenched, as he pulls at my arm, shrouding furtive whispers, "We must leave…I told you this would happen!" Change the room around, put this chair over there and move this one to that side. You're exhausting us, Dad, his son kidded. Help him eat, help him to the commode, hold the hand that has no grasp, call the nurse, he's watching something cross the room, "What's going on here," he whispers. His eyes roll as his back arches violently in a slide from the bed to the floor. The tube has been pulled again. His nurse grabs my shoulders, and just inches from my stunned gaze, stares through me, as if shouting down an empty well: "He's had a seizure, he's…OK…he's OK." I'm sure those are the words she used.

On a good day we walk to the smoking area, a small room down the hall, unseen by outsiders, "set aside," he would monotone, "for the ones with nothing left." The tiny room is cluttered, unclean, like a bus station at the end of the day with butts mounded in the ashtray, no ventilation, the foulness its own deadening enclosure. He inhales deeply, staring across the rooftop into an *elsewhere.* I'm dismissed, an outsider, watching pigeons flutter from the ledges in April's sunny air; a meadow across the road is about to burst with green, hope hostage to vacuum.

His coughing wanes as the three of us, his IV pole between, scuff slowly to our accommodation, a bed and a lounge chair. Robin will come in the morning to sit with her father while I drive home to catch up on the mundane, to move about on the outside. The days smear into numbing ritual—feed the cat, open the mail, write a check, call family and friends who want to be useful, tell them "he's doing fine…one day at a time…as well as he can be…"

Then back to the room, to *It*. No longer my husband, the wit, the lover, my friend, the entrepreneur, the alcoholic who intended to escape the tailspin, get control, but without the meetings, not his "vehicle…alcoholism a state of mind, no different than overeating, only a matter of resolve." He would make up his mind one day and just quit "…tomorrow, after the weekend, after the business is sold… soon…when the dust settles…when the dust settles." After the dust settles.

"One day at a time…good days, bad days." On his fiftieth birthday, home-town pals gather around his bed. It's been a *good day* and he sits like a chairman of the board, basking in a fragile glow, certain to evaporate almost at once. They laugh at the old days, the hangout on Main Street, now gone, of hot rods, skipping school, of Latin *ad infinitum* and bagging groceries at the A&P, a jittery class reunion—the final "…take care…see ya later."

His contact with the outside world ended abruptly, another chapter closed, another anguished descent along a darkened stairway. "Put a sign on the door, family only. Tell them I'm sleeping." He would never see *outsiders* again. We've been here four weeks now, and each day something worsens. His urine is orange; now there's fluid in his lungs, they're tying him down. Please help me, my brain screams, flailing on emotional fly paper, the days are lost, time derailed. Tears won't come. When will I cry?

It happened somewhere near the end of those days, the final act on a stage of shadows, his torment more desperate somehow from a man known for his control, who was nothing if not in charge. Seated in a wheelchair, he clutched at my arm, his skin cold with sweat, his hands twisting at my clothes, rocking in my embrace, pulling at my shirt, twisting its fabric, his soul erupting with terror as people in the hall turn slowly our way, silhouettes in a ghastly fluorescent haze, mute audience to his cries, choking cries from a child who has cried too long, or not enough…"I want to die…just let me go! I don't want to die!"

It was the quiet that morning, the stillness. The dawn quiet when hospital energy takes pause, and it crushed the air. I and his son seemed to jolt from momentary sleep at once, glancing across his bed, looking at each other, not yet at him. The silence hung like wet wool, its foul weight holding me against the chair, as if stifling movement would rectify a vague discomfort. His struggle for breath, each one so deliberate, so exhausting throughout the long night had stopped. The night nurse embraced us both. Rich went to make phone calls, and the nurse turned to me again, saying that when death has recently occurred, she believed that communication might be possible across "the gap." She closed the door quietly behind her, and I exhaled a prayer. It was over, his life in limbo, his suffering at an end. I held his hand, staring numbly into his brown eyes, once so mischievous, once so focused and smart. Above so much else, smart. I studied his gaze, unable to speak one last time, unable to think or cry, as if time outside that room had continued and we had ceased together, language impossible.

My emotional remains were swept through the days to come— arrangements, calling hours, embraces, words of love, words of assurance, kindly smiles…he was so strong…he looks so at peace now… giddy remembrances of the old days, the elders still calling him Jimmy. "If there's anything I can do…"

The rain that week was apt theater for the tears that would finally come. I dug into the herb garden. Thyme and the lush green of spring's grass intensified with the rain, no one would see, the rain too heavy, as folds of the yellow slicker formed rivers across my face while the sky and my spirit drenched.

Healing, recovery, going it alone: another chapter. I visit his grave with roses. Are they all there watching me, as in *Our Town*, the dead, talking among themselves of eternity, as they "wait for the eternal part in them to come out clear?" Is he serene in that other place?

Is he smiling, forgiving my shredded attentions those last months? Does he know that love was there among the shreds?

On the second anniversary of his death to lymphoma, a malignancy of the immune system, Hollywood's highly acclaimed film and the soundtrack to go with it, holds a lyrical mirror to that dismal corridor with words Jim uttered in similar despair:

> *"Saw my reflection in a window and didn't know my own face...can feel myself fading away...at night I could hear the blood in my veins...just as black and whispering as the rain..."*
>
> —Bruce Springsteen,
> "Streets of Philadelphia"

CHAPTER 4

The Window's Open

Jim's death ended our seven-year marriage, the second for both of us. Our successful convenience store business had been sold the year before, and friends who owned a weekly newspaper offered part-time work, my first desk job in seven years. Simply put, working at the paper was life in college, and let's not forget the thrill of owning and operating a business 24/7 with my spouse for six years prior to that—easier to smile at, given time.

Elsewhere, as yet unrealized, were the makings of a plan. Larry McMurtry's Pulitzer Prize-winning tale of the vanishing west, *Lonesome Dove,* triggered the awakening. In the space of four nights, 1989's TV miniseries progressively summoned Wilfred Hathaway's daughter to leave her house, as did the novel in a subsequent, spell-binding read.

Have you thought about what's ahead, Gloria Jean? The window's open. You're on your own. You could drive alone to the middle of nowhere like John Steinbeck, but without the dog, like July Johnson through these pages, looking for something he's not sure he'll find. There's no reason not to, the pages counseled. I know you can! I know you can! You survived that wrong turn in Florida, you can find Montana. You're a Hathaway, as in Wilfred.

The next prompt came disguised as a sympathy card from friends: *The Master Weaver*

> *Our lives are but fine weavings*
> *that God and we prepare,*

19

Each life becomes a fabric planned
and fashioned in His care.
We may not always see just how
the weavings intertwine,
But we must trust the Master's hand
and follow His design,
For He can view the pattern
upon the upper side,
While we must look from underneath
and trust in Him to guide.
Sometimes a strand of sorrow
is added to His plan,
And though it's difficult for us,
we still must understand
That it's He who fills the shuttle,
it's He who knows what's best,
So we must weave in patience
and leave to Him the rest.
Not 'til the loom is silent
and the shuttles cease to fly
Shall God unroll the canvas
and explain the reason why—
The dark threads are as needed
in the Weaver's skillful hand
As the threads of gold and silver
in the pattern He has planned.

Messages seemed to arrive in daily epiphanies. Magazines, newspapers, even the occasional billboard offered random insight— my soul had opened, so even the word *Go* was absorbed as cosmic advice. Horoscopes had their say, and when the spirit is vacant, who hasn't latched on to a totally relevant message from the stars? Then came Oprah one afternoon as I lay cemented to the sofa, grieving widow succumbed to inertia. The topic of the show involved taking control: *"Women Without Focus, Today's Oprah."*

"If you do what you've always done, you'll get what you've always gotten. Make a list," she advised, "Ten things: Where do you want to go in life? If you could do anything in the years to come, what must be done to achieve it? How long will it take? How to finance it? Who's stopping you, now or years from now, what's stopping you? Make your list. What's really holding you back?" *Well, probably nothing, Oprah. Probably nothing…I think.*

The vision mushroomed. The plan became the dream, the dream became the itinerary, the wall map, the file box, lists, letters to future destinations for travel info, maps to study, homework: "Better English Made Easy." Pandora slides along the avalanche.

Introducing my plan to the world was its own journey, not the sort of thing a *woman my age* does without *companionship.* Most often the reaction was a vacant, *you're-not-serious* expression, but after I described the idea and the concept seemed almost real, came the monotone: *Oh, wow, that sounds great…let me know how it goes… So how are plans coming for the trip? When is it you're going again? Can't you find someone to go with you? Oh, you should bring a dog, like that guy with the poodle.* I'm convinced that few thought this odyssey would ever come about, but I learned to dismiss the negatives, or at least work through it with some inner condescension of my own— ruminating, is it?

"That guy with the poodle?" That guy? Someone to go with me? How would that work? Whose journey would that be? I'm Wilfred's kid, it's in my genes, and with or without a dog this journey west is going to happen! Hair brained, nutty, cockamamie, perhaps, but it's not Mt. Everest. It's a drive in a freakin' car!

CHAPTER 5

And Now a Word from James Joyce

Midnight makes it official—1994 has come to pass. Fireworks echo across the valley from a neighboring town as Orion dances through the night across frozen snow, a luminous upheaval shoved along the street in thick moonlit slabs. The *Great Hunter* hurdles the house in stride, instigating courage in my restive soul; we're headed for dawn, headed for the summer of '96.

Tomorrow the wall map will go up, a 24 x 36 *USA* tucked in an issue of National Geographic, a so-called *Landsat* version—satellite imagery in shades of green; darker green for urban areas and pale gold for thin vegetation, desert shrubland, and plowed cropland. A route of string will be affixed, beginning here in southern New Hampshire, north to the Canadian border, west to Ohio, to Michigan, Dakota and Montana; then south to Texas and home via Orient Point, Long Island, where 'Travels' began with Charley. A plastic milk crate left over from

the store will work nicely as a portable file drawer with hanging folders, one for each state to be crossed.

To stand on a prairie and see nothing; will my future *Letters from the Road* get published? Is that even possible? Will it matter if they're not? Is it enough to just do it? Over and over the wonder as the unrelenting dream weaves its pathway west. First stop: Pittsburg, NH to photograph moose sipping the bog in late afternoon. And where will I first encounter bison? What about tornadoes? Are there guidelines for that beyond *watch out?* What writing will come from a *plains* room in the middle of nowhere? Where *is* the middle of nowhere? What will be the news as I pass through Hope, Arkansas, election year '96? And who might be in line with me at Graceland on that August night in Memphis, the nineteenth anniversary of *The King's* passing? A tantalizing expectation, these friends as yet unmet, and where they might be from. Will I find Wilma's name in the Baseball Hall of Fame? Or stand in Lake Superior's storied icy water? If I reach Hathaway, Montana, will I find an insulator there? And the lure of Prairie Rose, North Dakota, no other reason for passing through than the pure charm of its name. Will it be as I've imagined? Wounded Knee in South Dakota—what are the words to come? Is this really going to happen? I shared the plan with a few friends this week, and I would guess they're muttering to themselves, *still grieving…it'll pass.*

Hindsight: The following moment of clarity was brought to me by James Joyce in his short story masterpiece, *The Dead*: "Better to pass boldly into that other world in the full glory of some passion, than fade and wither dismally with age."

"Better to pass boldly into that other world in the full glory of some passion, than fade and wither dismally with age." Right on, Mr. Joyce, right on!

*****

GLORIA JEAN

The Itinerary
Memorial Day to Labor Day, 1996

Memorial Day, Concord to Pittsburg—the moose at dusk await;
O'er top Vermont and across Champlain, the first big lake
Down to Wilma's *"League of Her Own"* at
baseball's *Hall* in Cooperstown,
From the tips of the Fingerlakes to Niagara, the *first* Buffalo
Lake Erie's *Hall*: Absolute R & R
Lake Superior—*The Wreck of the Edmund
Fitzgerald*—homage at Whitefish;
Wisconsin's forehead to Minnesota's twin cities
North to Fargo/Moorehead, the other twins;
The sweet oasis of Prairie Rose, a drift through Dakota's space
The middle of nowhere—photographs, sketches, notes
Here and there a church sermon, main street diners
Laundromats, local color from the radio,
small town, front-page news
Church suppers, grange meetings, front porches
Letters home from plains rooms
Lonesome Dove reaches Miles City
South to Hathaway seeking one more insulator for Dad
To the Little Bighorn
Fourth of July at Belle Fourche
The Black Hills, past Rushmore's faces
Crazy Horse to Wounded Knee
North Platte, Chimney Rock, the ruts of the Oregon Trail
Dodge to Oklahoma City's *Hall of Cowboys*
Emory, Texas—time with old friends
Watch the Democratic Convention in Hope, Arkansas
Memphis—Beale Street to Graceland
The battlefield at Antietam's River
The Wall
Good-bye to an old friend in Annapolis
Brooklyn's Bridge at dawn

To Orient Point where 'Travels' began with
Charley—homage to Mr. Steinbeck
Ferry to New London, Block Island and Pt. Judith
In the Great State of Rhode Island and Providence Plantations
To Elm Grove Cemetery with the insulator
for Wilfred Hathaway's grave
*"Go confidently in the direction of your dreams. Live the
life you have imagined."* Reflections at Walden Pond
Home, Labor Day

"Better to pass boldly into that other world in the full glory of some passion, than
fade and wither dismally with age."—James Joyce, "The Dead"

CHAPTER 6

Oh, *That* Darkness!

Golda Meow dismissed herself from my bed, her sleep most likely interrupted by the sounds pushing in twisted syllables from my throat as I tried to scream. Her feet hit the oak floor with a familiar muffled thud, punctuating the nightmare I struggled to escape. I lay cemented to the pillow, breathless, as yet not fully awake.

I'd found myself on a dark backstreet, held to the hands of strangers, eyes that stare past my own to another room, no way to communicate with or to them. Their being, that life, which has swept them here is far from my own, mute horrid faces, all of them ghosts finishing out their time, hovering in shadows, caught in nets, large blackened fingers clutching, never letting them go from that *Last Exit to*...whatever city I was walking with my daughter Michele and my son, the two Peters, one the toddler, and the other, his adolescent brooding self. It may have been Boston, as glimpses of the expressway appear in quick fades.

We were leaving a large public arena, walking an underground concourse to the car. Peter, the young adult, was laughing and clowning less than Michele and I, he more concerned with getting there, impatient as usual. Dread hung over me, and each time I looked back at Peter, concerned he wasn't carrying the other, toddling Peter, the baby boy who crept through my mind of late. As the walk grew longer I worried more that the baby couldn't keep up, that Peter wasn't watching him.

There's confusion; we were separated. I couldn't find Michele, and not long afterward, I saw her lying at the side of the highway, cars rushing by, and when the ambulance arrived, no one seemed concerned; they moved in slow motion. She wasn't moving, they were taking her to a hospital, but I had to get back to the car and find Peter. I rushed through alleys searching, combing the sidewalks, searching, searching. Now it was dark, and each corner brought me into the shadows, dank glistening streets, terror stalking, no one offering to help, no one there but for cold, evil gargoyles turning my way at each corner. I came out on a rooftop, a parking garage, I think, but with no walls; it must have been midnight, deserted, dank black with a stifling web of fog. I was startled by a presence, a tall, menacing man-woman with dark circles around its empty eyes, staring through me, zombie-like. I wanted to leave and it grabbed my hands. I was backing toward the edge of the roof. It turned quickly, tugging at a grimy casket offered from the shadows. I worried about Peter and the baby and remembered Michele's sunlit curls spread across the expressway, gleaming gold about her stillness. Where is she? Who will worry about them now? That's when Golda Meow hit the floor with a thud.

Sigmund Freud aside, I believe the "Spirit of Christmas Future" had paid me a metaphorical visit, never speaking, its bony hand gesturing to the grave in silent foreboding, the presence on the roof conveying its voiceless dread, surely a lesson in terror from the *Master Weaver*—caution, common sense.

*****

↗ **SAGITTARIUS:** The moon in your own birth sign on Tuesday means you must now summon up the courage to do what you should have done about six months ago. Everything you are now experiencing is merely clearing a path so that something more worthwhile can come through.

—TV Guide

Too often we are scared.
Scared of what we might not be able to do.
Scared of what people might think if we tried.
We let our fears stand in the way of our hopes.
We say no when we want to say yes.
We sit quietly when we want to scream.
And we shout with the others,
When we should keep our mouths shut.
Why?
After all, we do only go around once.
There's really no time to be afraid.
So stop!
Try something you've never tried. Risk it.
Enter a triathlon.
Write a letter to the editor.
Demand a raise.
Call winners at the toughest court.
Throw away your television.
Bicycle across the United States.
Try bobsledding.
Try anything.
Speak out against the designated hitter.
Travel to a country where you don't speak the language.
Patent something.
Make that call…
You have nothing to lose,
And everything, everything, everything to gain.
Just do it!

—Nike ad

CHAPTER 7

The Prequel

January, 1995; Department of Tourism, Pierre, South Dakota: I am in the process of planning a three-month drive in the summer of '96 from my home in central New Hampshire, across northern boundaries to Miles City, Montana, south past Rushmore and Crazy Horse to the Dallas area, and back east via Arkansas, Kentucky, and Maryland. An itinerary is enclosed, and I would welcome any suggestions you might have regarding advance contacts—local news, ranching communities, etc., and where accommodations are concerned, I am looking for the most basic of rooms, including a night or two in someone's barn…etc. etc…*Ditto: Montana, Wyoming, Nebraska, Oklahoma, Texas, etc.*

March, 1996; Editor, *City Paper*: For more than two years I have been formulating plans for a solitary odyssey to the heartland and home. It will…

Dear Mr. Editor: It will be a journey to outer space, a woman alone in middle age…Specifically, what I propose is a weekly corner on travel, directed for the most part at women in my fifty-plus age group…a good-humored focus on small-town, back-road news, climate, politics, and other daily surprises…from diners to lodging cheap; the possibilities are tantalizing. After three months of planning, the vision continues to take on a life of its own…headed for nowhere, the middle of it, alone…

———————

Travel Editor: It will be an odyssey to the Heartland and home, a quest for the *middle of nowhere*. My once and future *Letters from the Road* will explore the notion of weaving unhurried through another valley alone, beginning in Concord on Memorial Day 1996, concluding roughly six thousand miles and twenty-six states later on Labor Day weekend…In two months, the journey will begin and I would be very interested in discussing this project with you…itinerary and writing sample enclosed…

———————

Postmaster, Hathaway, Montana: You will see on the enclosed itinerary that I plan an extended journey next summer, driving roughly six thousand miles in three months. Several factors have brought me to this point, uppermost my love for writing and an inherited passion for reading maps and driving to parts unknown. My father drove most of this country in a camper, including Alaska and much of Canada, and across the miles he collected glass insulators. When he died ten years ago, he had accumulated more than three hundred, and I saved one of each color. So you might understand that throughout my own journey I plan to find one more insulator to place at his grave, at Wilfred Hathaway's grave, and beyond that, my excitement at finding the town of Hathaway directly along my intended route. With that in mind, I wonder if you could supply me with the name of a rooming house in your area I could contact in advance. Many thanks for any information you might provide…self-addressed envelope enclosed.

*****

All in the State of Mind

What will I do when the letter arrives, or the phone call from *City Paper* and there's an absence of interest? Or if nothing arrives at all? Will it all crash? How to prepare? Coach Keaney's words echo across thirty years: *"If you think you are beaten, you are; If you think you dare not, you won't; if you'd like to win, but think you can't, it's almost a cinch you won't..."* But the force continues...do it anyway...the rest will take care of itself...what's to lose? Just do it! *"Full many a coward fails, ere ever his work's begun; success begins with a fellow's will, it's all in the state of mind..."*

If I don't do this with every inch of grit, with whatever it takes, what then, what *will* I do? Continue working at the paper? How long? What then? I know what's going on here. I'm doing what all the old folks did on *The Simpsons* when they were liberated en masse from the Springfield Retirement Castle, when they all tottered to the front door, cheering, "We're free, we can leave..." then stopped short, with whatever reason could be found to stay, turning around en masse, muttering, "I'm hungry...it's time for my nap...it's too hot." That's what I'm doing. Years from now, will I remember this specific moment in time? Will I have spent thirty or forty more years wishing I were somewhere else? *Do you have what it takes, Gloria Jean? Did this whole notion, this Letters from the Road thing, plant itself in your soul three years ago as a pipe dream? Is it naptime, Gloria Jean? Too hot? Time for supper? Will all of this crumble in the shadow of some vague fear or because one editor lacks interest?* **"If you think you're outclassed, you are; you've got to think high to rise..."** *James Joyce stepped into your road for a reason: "Better to pass boldly into that other world in the full glory of some passion than fade and wither dismally with age."*

Here's how it works: get off your petrified ass and do it! Just do it! There are words to come from the Middle of Nowhere. **"Life's battles don't always go to the stronger or faster man...but sooner or later the man who wins is the fellow who thinks he can!"**

♐ **SAGITTARIUS:** Whatever projects you've been hatching recently, now is the time to begin putting them into operation, while both the sun and Mars form such a beneficial aspect to Saturn in Aquarius. Above all, don't be put off by others' cynicism or lack of faith. If you can imagine it, you can achieve it.

—TV Guide

31

One Month to Liftoff, April 1996

There it is again, here in the middle of my road, this savage stage fright. *What are you thinking? What can come of it? You can't really believe this is going to end well. It would be different if you were **somebody**. John Steinbeck **was** somebody! "Travels with Charley" for God's sake! You're not a real writer. You're a dilettante, a damned fool! And listen to the news; there's evil out there, murder in random roulette. Remember that hideous nightmare? You could vanish from sight in some remote place and never be found. What about your family? Have you thought about how this might affect them? Who really supports any of this? What will happen when you come back—if you come back? Why can't you be like other women your age...never seem to fit the mold. Settle down. Get a job.*

—Signed, Regular Folks

*****

Oh, **that** Panic Attack!

I'm under siege, it seems. My recent viewing of *Jurassic Park* surely triggered this latest terror, a raptor stalking me at every corner till I could struggle no longer; waking in a cold sweat. The journey ahead is too big, too overwhelming. I can't do this, but neither can I back out. How would I do that? Would I lie, make up some terrible affliction? What would that be? How about a nervous breakdown? That would do it. Tuck me away in an empty room and watch as I stare mutely past all the regular folks into another world, the world I will never see **because I chickened out on this trip!**

Who can I share this with? My daughter would listen, my cheerleading daughter, the one who encouraged me every step over the past three years, the one I'm setting this *courageous* example for, planning, following through. Am I going to suggest to her that this adventure won't be taken? *Can't* be taken? What would that do to her alone, much less anyone else? People like Pat and Gordon, who never questioned the wisdom of doing the trip, always encouraging and supportive. Michele senses this hesitation anyway. I've felt it coming. She knows I'm backpedalling. The conversation will surface soon. I describe my Jurassic sequence, the terror of it, making the obvious interpretation to this *Psychology Today* reader. I'm not stupid, Michele. It's not a dinosaur I fear, it's the Rand McNally gorilla, and I'm going to fall flat on my ass! But I can't *not* go now! That's what they expect; they've known it all along; it's too far-fetched. *"A woman your age…whew! She's finally come to her senses! Here, read the want ads, you'll find a job soon."*

Then it comes back to me…are you going to "fade and wither… fade and wither dismally"…like those folks in the home featured on the front page of *City Paper* last week, lined up in wheelchairs along the hall? I'm better now. Jim would be applauding this, probably even more than Michele is. The missing man in my life, the man who fought the odds in a way I never thought possible, a prisoner, six years in a bleak terminal. But I'm convinced he left this planet proud that he'd won some battles, too stubborn to ever admit the disease got the best of him. He died of something else, his heart stopped; it wasn't the cancer—inspiration from the grave. This was only one more jitter. I'll be fine. *Think on your feet,* came Jim's soft murmur, *Think on your feet.*

> "In long-range planning for a trip, I think there is a private conviction that it won't happen. As the day approached, my warm bed and comfortable house grew increasingly desirable and my dear wife incalculably precious. To give these up for three months for the terrors of the uncomfortable and unknown seemed crazy. I didn't want to go. Something had to happen to forbid my going, but it didn't."
>
> —John Steinbeck
> *Travels with Charley: In Search of America*

CHAPTER 8

Flashback: Brought to You in Living Black and White

In 1959, girls not destined for college got a job straight out of high school, and the business curriculum was pretty much the way to go—bookkeeping, shorthand, typing—talk about dinosaurs.

Time-Out! That's typing, *not* keyboarding. If you earned your high school diploma in the nineties and beyond, you might as well skip the following paragraphs; go ahead, single file, no chortling. At the dawn of time we learned how to type on *manual* typewriters. Remember them, girls? Remember the classroom filled with Royals, Underwoods, Remingtons, and Smith Coronas chattering like insects in the dead of night? Close your eyes: both thumbs on the space bar, beginning with the left pinky: *a-s-d-f space;* right pinky: *;-l-k-j.* Again and again, practice, practice, over and over; the thrill of speed tests, preparing us for the civil service exam in Providence and a future state job. The gentleman with the stopwatch spoke firmly: "Begin." He might well have blasted a large cannon for the mind-blowing level of stress it produced, as the sound of fifteen or twenty machines began to hammer in riotous disharmony—pounding keys, tiny bells chiming, carriage returns slamming, he pacing the aisles, watching his watch to the bloody end. "Time is up," he monotoned. Would I qualify for employment at my future of choice? I waited for the good news to arrive days later, delivered in the mail by a *snail.*

As it turned out, my *Clerk Typist* status with the State of Rhode Island was official; all that remained was an actual job interview when

URI's August summons arrived: *Please report to the Personnel Office, Davis Hall, re: Clerk Typist position, Professor Frederic D. Tootell, Director of Athletics and Chairman of the Department of Physical Education for Men.*

The boys' gym needed a secretary? What for? How would *Senior Office Practice* have rehearsed telephone etiquette for this... business? I rehearsed diction and telephone manner: *Good morning, Department of Athletics and Physical Education for Men.* My inner adolescent considered "*Jocks and Socks, go, Rams!*"

Having procured credentials from *Personnel*, I left the administration building and headed for Keaney Gym as instructed, "down the hill, just off campus." The summer quadrangle was noticeably deserted, scattered with only a few couples *lounging* under the elms. *Just off campus* soon manifested itself when the approach to a distant gymnasium was at hand. My appropriate medium-heeled shoes stood at the apex. Descending mesas of concrete steps cascaded before me, leveling off midway to accommodate a dormitory complex. Continuing across an access road, I passed the front door of the infirmary, an ironic pit stop to the citadel of physical fitness. The narrow path turned to blacktop, extending in a charcoal carpet for the final stretch, shaded on either side with a tunnel of foliage. I pictured my car parked at Davis Hall, wishing to thank Miss Doran for her *just off campus* directions. The Aggie Barn, beyond the football stadium, cast an odorous reminder of its presence while Keaney Gymnasium stood before me, its brick façade flat against the sky and a row of glass doors that screamed with morning sun, mirroring in my shadow the water tower "just off campus," which suggested at that moment an exclamation point. Six empty flag poles rattled across the roof with metallic clamor, applauding my arrival in August's breeze.

My footsteps echoed across the lobby on terrazzo flooring that held an inlaid seal of the university. Ticket booths flanked either side, leading to a lobby and another strip of doors to the main gymnasium, its floor gleaming with fresh varnish. Shuffling feet came from a corridor to my right, someone limping, pushing toward me with a yard-wide dust mop. A grimy baseball cap shaded bushy gray eyebrows and wire-rimmed glasses, and he wore two, maybe three shirts, the top one a gray *URI* sweatshirt, dark wool trousers, and flapping black shoes that kept rhythm with jangling keys. Unshaven, chewing a day-old cigar, drooling slightly from the corners of a wide grin, his eyes twinkled at the chance to be of help. "Mornin', miss," he cackled. "You're bright 'n early. Lookin' for someone special or just vistin'? If you're going to be here this fall, I think you got the wrong gym. This is the boys' gym. The girls' gym is back up on campus."

The wrong gym? *The wrong gym?* But I was sure she spoke the words *Keaney Gymnasium* and, one more time, *down the hill, just off campus.* "I have an appointment with Mr. Tootell, and…" "Oh, he's here all right, right down this hall." George Draper's wide mop led the way to a small office. "Ya know, afta school starts I have to buff these corridors ever day." "Oh?" "Oh, yesh! This red tile scuffs real easy and the chief likes it shining. Nothin' but the best for Toot!" I followed his shuffle, walking to the cadence of fifteen or twenty keys pounding against his hip.

My obliging guide offered a *Keaney Blue* chair in the reception area as he quickly scuffed down another hall to find his chief. Venetian blinds rattled against the open window beside a vacant desk, its electric typewriter neatly covered with a contoured blanket. Papers were held in place by a miniature *Rodin,* one hand folded against his chin, the other resting across his knee, pondering his nudity and the fluttering stack beneath. A larger office sat empty in the next room, its desk mounded with paper. A few minutes had passed when an eerie, vibrating rumble came from the hall beyond, loud at first, then nearly inaudible, bizarre, indecipherable. As it grew closer, I heard it as singing. That was it, a deep voice was singing, or was it voices? It reverberated through the hall like Gregorian chant. A choir of monks in the boys' gym? Doors opened and slammed nearby, announcing the immediate entrance of a behemoth. Dressed in navy blue gym shorts and a polo shirt, his bronze balding head barely cleared the doorway as hairy suntanned arms reached out to dislodge my shoulder with a handshake. A Papa Bear voice rose from size-huge tennis shoes. "I'm a bit underdressed for an interview, but come on in." He chuckled softly. Was this "Toot"?

Stacks of paper were mimeographed or duplicated (as in purple ditto masters) but mostly handwritten sheets of yellow lined paper that covered the desk. He seemed ill at ease as I imagined a crane lowering his frame into the chair, fumbling through some sheets for something it seemed he'd never find, so I offered my credentials that he scanned with a soft la la la. I wondered why his glasses were strapped to his face with black elastic bands, one side slipping a bit, "Your glasses…" "Uh…ha! Lester's on vacation now, and he usually does all my hiring, but here's a short letter I've got to get out. He gave me a handwritten sheet. "You can use Sue's typewriter out there, she's on vacation too."

Waiting for him to check my work was like waiting for a phone to ring, and I wished one would, just to see how he might answer. He cleared his throat. "Uh, there's a semicolon missing here in paragraph two, but I don't think anyone will notice. He signed the memo, official confirmation: Frederic D. Tootell, Director of Athletics.

Elbows on the desk, fingers woven beneath his chin, his eyes crinkled above a toothy smile. "Uh,"—he spoke like John Wayne—"ya know, you young gals are OK, but after two or three years you run off and get married on us." I mentally sentenced myself: five to ten in the boys' gym. "Can ya come back next week and meet Lester? He'll be back from vacation and will fill you in on things. How about Wednesday?" "What time?" "Oh, whenever you get here in the mornin' will be fine." He grabbed a tennis racket and rose to leave with another chuckle. "You'll be on the payroll the twenty-fourth," he boomed, and his bass voice trailed beyond slamming doors, echoing the mysterious melody I would hear so many times through that corridor in URI's Department of Physical Education for Men and Intercollegiate Athletics, a hard-to-top first job for a *young lady*, age eighteen, fresh out of school, but that's for another telling although the following brief recollection belongs to the ages. In the winter of 1960, on the morning after a heavy snowstorm, which most commuters might use as an excuse to remain buried at home, I took great pride in having showed up—ever dressed for the office—thinking it would greatly impress Boss Tootell. He handed me a shovel, and we both cleared snow from Keaney Gymnasium's expansive winter apron.

> **Hindsight:** *"With a toss of 174' 10-1/8," world record holder Frederic Delmont Tootell (Bowdoin College, '23) was the first American-born winner of the Olympic hammer throw, 1924 Paris Olympics."*

*****

In 1960 the Eisenhower years closed with the dawn of *Camelot*, the *Jackie Era*—bouffant hair, skirts hemmed just below the knee, oh, and pearls. At bedtime our heads containing six or eight brush rollers hung in the air from a pillow sculpted between the neck and shoulder, said curlers not pressing into the scalp.

The *IBM Selectric* typewriter set a new secretarial pace; however, letters and reports using carbon paper and onionskin were corrected with erasers on sticks topped with little brushes for whisking the crumbs—"delete" as yet unrealized in the clerical middle ages. Carbon copies required small pieces of torn paper tucked behind each carbon sheet to mask the smudge when erasing. We mimeographed, collated, and stapled, but who's complaining? The whippersnapper who's reading this in spite of my instructions missed out on some basic character building—broken nails, stiff necks, a fortune in hosiery, and wayward blobs of mimeograph ink dotting our gray flannel straight skirts. All you do now is press *Enter, Delete,* or *Esc* while that machine in the other room sorts, folds and staples. Where's the discipline in that? I'll tell you where: it's in Camelot, plum faded away, along with stencils and correction fluid—an interesting fragrance, by the way, reminiscent of ether.

We got married, quit work, and had a couple of kids. Elvis joined the army while prehistoric computers the size of a large room keypunched us to the seventies. The jolt of Kennedy's assassination came and went, along with *Laugh-In, Bonnie and Clyde,* the Beatles, Woodstock, and Vietnam. Then came *Ms. Magazine* and women in a brand new workplace—typewriters no longer happening, computers now and the *agony of delete.*

CHAPTER 9

The White Rabbit

I'm exactly one month from liftoff, my employment at *the Suncook Valley Sun* nearly over—graduation from Word Processing 101. Where else would I have hooked up with *Ctrl, Alt,* and *Delete* but for these friends who brought me into it hands-on? "The only way to learn is to do it," they said. I've thought many times over, I should have paid *them* for the experience.

It's 8:00 am; I'm about to leave for work as a traffic jam occurs in front of the house. School traffic is usually the reason as cars line up behind a bus, but the line this day was longer than usual, slower moving, probably a fender bender. But then it appeared, a young moose standing amid the obliging cars, befuddled, at one moment facing north, ignoring the vehicles around him, unsure of where to turn; then, looking behind, as if for a signal, he turned and headed for my yard, his head raised slightly, loping across the lawn toward the back meadow. The first moose I'd ever seen in the flesh, here in the *burbs*, showing up at this precise moment, stopping traffic precisely in front of my specific house! The moose glanced my way, a siren to the north woods, *it's on*

your itinerary, he winked, the first line: if you drive there, we will come. Master Weaver's green flag gave a loud snap.

That evening I stood in the herb garden savoring a splendid peace, remembering the handsome mooseling of mottled brown cantering across my field in the morning sun, his feet crackling into the woods beyond, out of sight, like the white rabbit enticing Alice to follow. Scanning the tree line, I wondered where he was at this sunset, wishing for another sighting. Something flapped in the breeze from a small tree that stood alone in the field like a halfhearted flagpole, a maple about twenty feet tall. It held a piece of cloth snagged on a short branch, clearly a reason to move closer to the woods. The cloth turned out to be a plastic kite, white with a brown design, and when I pulled it from the branch to spread it before me, a dinosaur, Tyrannosaurus Rex, roared from the plastic, its eyes red, words magic-marked across its muscular chest: *Just do it*, it smiled. *Just do it!*

Michele, possibly the *Master Weaver* in cahoots.

CHAPTER 10

"But be prepared to bleed."
—Joni Mitchell

So! This is hell week! Due to a lack of interest, I was turned down by the travel editor at *City Paper*. The map on the wall stares me in the face. My writing sample is "too train of thought," said the phone voice, a young man, thirtyish, maybe. It wouldn't work as a weekly column. I'm not known. Did three years of focus, all the planning, hinge on one person? I'm a rat now, pacing the labyrinth, staring at the map. What should happen, or what shouldn't? This can't all have been for nothing. "Too train of thought." What the hell does that mean, Travel Boy? How old are you, twelve? Over and over, I've said it: the success or failure of this doesn't depend on *them*. But that's what this crying jag is all about, this candle-burning, wine-wallowing performance. Travel Guy said no; get back in the swarm.

But what did Oprah say, and James Joyce? Should I be ignoring James Joyce? Or that dinosaur on the kite, the moose in the road, all those horoscopes? Who's ushering your fate, a twelve-year-old? After the knockdowns, a deep breath, a good night's sleep, the surge remains, the motor rumbles, waiting for the flag. Looking down the barrel of age 55, all the negatives merely gnats. Today's ***Final Jeopardy***: What is "Nothing to Lose?"

♐ **SAGITTARIUS:** Because your ruler, Jupiter, teams up with the Sun on the eighteenth, no door can remain locked or barred for long. In fact, if a plan or project close to your heart was given the thumbs-down by those in positions of power recently, now is the ideal time to try again. This time, simply refuse to take no for an answer.

—TV Guide

CHAPTER 11

Moody Feline Seeks Temporary Summer Lodging—Not!

Golda Meow has shared my space since her adoption from the Humane Society ten years ago, the only kitten on death row not stretching its paws through the wire or meowing pathetically at the cage door, instead sitting smugly at the back of her small enclosure, expecting to be chosen.

Now comes my little trip and what to do with *Queen of the House* for three months. Michele offered her apartment in town as temporary quarters, the perfect solution—for *me*. Golda, on the other hand must now endure summer camp with another cat, even worse, a rowdy adolescent. Today is the day of deliverance, which begs the question: when it's over in three months, will she have forgotten me?

First, there's her disdain for the so-called *Easy-Tote Pet Taxi*, a cardboard box secured with interlocking flaps, pierced with breathing holes, used mostly for routine visits to the vet, itself an event uncalled for. On first sight of the dreadful conveyance, her physical self achieves an altered state, a pitchfork struck by lightning, its steel tines twisted to opposite angles, all of them wider than the top of a pet taxi. She's Linda Blair without the green hurl, exorcism not an option. The conflict is routine, but once her imperious self is deposited within, Ms. Meow's scowl steams from the holes, and throughout the five-minute drive to the vet her guttural yowls attain alley cat status, always a startling serenade from ten pounds of house cat. But today's drive was quieter than most. Possibly our recent trip to the vet convinced her that such performance is wasted voice and best quietly endured.

Michele and I exchanged wary glances as the carrier was delivered to her specially prepared, upstairs urban residence. When I lowered the box and loosened the flaps, the expected orange blur catapulted from the stifling taxi. She stopped short, appearing confused. It wasn't home, but it wasn't the vet's. *What's this? No medicine smell, no slobbering mutts whining like tortured rabbits, no doctor voice saying what a nice old lady I am, poking, prodding, looking down my throat and other personal areas.* Her yellow eyes, halved across the top with heavy lids *a la* Garfield, magnifying the blackness of her large pupils as she turned my way, lifting her gaze to mine, radiating contempt: *Where **are** we, and **what** is going on?*

Her nose scanned the air, ignoring the wonderful bookcases with ample cat cubbies, or the sunny windowsills and bird audio wafting through the screens. With no warning, she turned and jumped back in the box, not a hint of pitchfork to the effort. Cat out-of-the-box, cat in-the-box! She'd have none of it, thank you very much, glaring from the shadows of the open flaps: *You can close the top now, Missy!*

Welcoming committee of one was Michele's cat Delilah, a juvenile Maine Coon with a mane of unruly fur puffing outwardly in explosive punk style that framed her tabby face, vertically divided through the center of her nose with a strip of beige, as though the gene police had used a rule. She was not at all pleased with the annoying screen placed across the doorway (recommended for seamless feline blending). Golda's pitiful meows came from beneath the bed, for her, a most unusual tone, as Delilah's hairy face moved urgently about in frantic stretches across the mesh barricade, her wide green eyes urging a response. *Come out here and show yourself, the world's a playground! Fat chance*, came the dark scowl, the scowl that didn't need to be seen.

Quote of the Day: "Mom, this is so sad." "It's not sad! It's not sad! Take the damn cat! It's only three months, she'll remember me—it's not sad!"

The angelic harmonies of Enya encouraged quiet tears between Michele's downtown *summer camp* and my soon to be vacated New Hampshire home. She'll be fine, my Golda Meow, scowling, growling, cranky cat, deigning to reside with *"Dumber."*

CHAPTER 12

Pack the Car

Milk Crate #1, Front Seat:
Rand McNally Road Atlas
Hanging folders, one for each state, in order of
appearance (state maps/tour guides)
"Road Whiz™ Plus," Hand-Held Interstate
Highway Guide from Trina (GPS, Primeval)

Milk Crate #2, Backseat Library:
NY Public Library Desk Reference, Dictionary,
Random House Desk Encyclopedia, "North American
Wildlife," "Quik-Reference, Essential Car Care"

Milk Crate #3, Backseat Office:
Empty pages, the yet-to-be-written diary
Canvas bag with portable word processor, floppy disks, paper,
pens, pencils, glue stick, scissors, ruler, paper clips, legal pads,
Small green three-ring binder for recording
mileage, meals, accommodations,
miscellaneous expenses;
Large green three-ring binder with calendar, itinerary, miscellaneous
references, credit card info, etc.

Other Necessities
Larger suitcase, later known as "the bureau in the trunk"
Smaller suitcase, "the overnighter"

Address / Phone Directory
Sunglasses
Key ring with personal ID info
Pepper Spray (directions included)
Trash Bag, Camera Bag, Purse
Family Photos (The Smile Book)
Radio / Emergency Flashing Light
Binoculars
Jackets, Sweaters, Hiking shoes

Travel Tokens:
The Rolling Soundtrack: "Letters from the Road"
Paperback "Lonesome Dove"
Little white dog from Sue, christened with St. Bernard spit
Travel mouse, named Christopher, with
brown knapsack from the *Mainers*
Crystal from Jan
Ziploc bags for Joey's cross country stone collection
Aunt Sam's Antique Bible, 1870 (several divinely
specific horoscopes taped inside)

♐ **SAGITTARIUS:** Current aspects indicate that a whole new chapter in your life is about to begin, so ally yourself to the forces of fate and set your sights as high as you can. To have faith is to have wings—and to have wings is to see things in perspective when everyone else is stumbling around in the dark.

—TV Guide

CHAPTER 13

Liftoff

Monday, May 27, 1996—Odometer 61,430

Waving a small New Hampshire flag from the car window, I left them in the driveway at 10:50 am. *Good-bye kids, I love you, please don't worry, I'm not crying...really.* I paste a picture of them in memory, the good-bye group, friends and family in front of my house standing beneath Memorial Day's flag. Gliding past the historic cemetery down the street, aging veterans salute the colors, dark uniforms with gold braid slide past, an old warrior facing the sun, saluting his flag, dress blues, tanned face, silver white hair gleaming against horn-rimmed glasses, shining brass, the silent Pembroke Street good-bye to Gloria Jean, forties period piece, license plate NH 12741, my Pearl

Harbor birth date only recognized now by the old soldiers of that war. The first fifty miles north on I-93 are surreal as Ted Hawkins wails "Candle in the Window," the first song on my soundtrack.

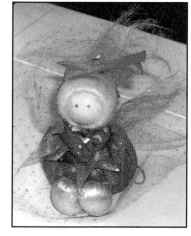

An assortment of good-luck gifts gained last minute entry into my car: a letter from my daughter, a letter "to be read later" from Arlene, my mother, and the bag "to be opened later" from Pat and Gordon. This was opened

140 miles later at a roadside sandwich stop outside Colebrook, lots of cheery little tokens for the journey ahead: a chubby angel with upswept yellow hair, sort of a cabbage patch midget with wings, a Lucy and Charlie Brown coffee mug with a note: "for when no other cup will do." Leave it to Pat, whom I nicknamed Lucy, always in my face about being strong, sticking to the dream. "Talk is cheap, block-head, get on with it!"

CHAPTER 14

New Hampshire

Monday and Tuesday, May 27, 28th
Spruce Cone Cabins and Campground, Pittsburg, NH—$50.00

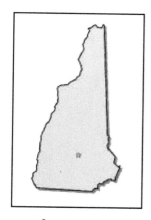

If New Hampshire's a wine bottle, I'm up here in the cork, and today's euphoria is brought to you from a back porch in Pittsburg, the upper deck of my first temporary residence. My feet rest on the rail overlooking Lake Francis, "…alone, alone, all all alone…" with it all before me.

It's 4:00 p.m. and a light breeze rustles the poplars that filter a view of the lake. A crow wobbles the top of a swaying spruce, a quiet space, except for the elderly couple sitting four units away at the far end of this porch, mollycoddling their Pomeranian, a rude carnival prize of a dog. He wears a coat the color of honey, and his pointed rodent nose threatens from the shadows of a chair. His bulging black eyes glare across the wood floor, lips curled back, exposing teeth in an absurd tiny smile, daring me to look his way. I pretend not to. We shadow glance, I look at him; he smiles savagely. I look away; he utters pitiful whines until I return the gaze. He smiles another snarl. Oh, if only I could beam him up, Scotty— Mack-back-home, the St. Bernard next door, although I've never seen him bare his teeth. He was a puppy when I first saw him, if St.

Bernards can be imagined in such a state. Sue and Joe had recently suffered the loss of Andre, their elderly Newfoundland and knew I had once owned a Saint. She stood at my door cradling her new baby, a teddy bear with chubby legs and fat paws draped loosely over her arm. He wore the classic black mask and a nose dotted with tiny freckles, a darling portent. "Kinda big for a little feller, ain't cha?" Aunt Sam might say. That was a year and a half ago.

I was shaking a small rug the other day when he caught my eye. The dog sat proudly beside his owner across the small field that separates our properties. He appeared to be sniffing the air for possibilities. Sue waved, carefully, painstakingly, because Mack was behaving, which is to say he wasn't dragging her across the earth. But then he spotted me, his devoted fan who doesn't mind the slobber, who brings him bones the size of a mailman's leg, and who yells

Hi, Mugwumps as he barks across the field from his porch. He decided at that moment to depart his vicinity for mine, and that his mom was holding the leash mattered little. She's short, trim, and sensible; she let it go. Imagine a small dog coming at you that hasn't seen its master in three hours, probably three weeks in dog mentality, but in the final sprint, the tiny animal morphs into a Harley. Mack's reddish brown mantle lumbered heavily across the straw field, ever revving, like a runaway cart loaded with fur pelts shifting to and fro as his flapping dog lips let go with tiny pearls of glistening drool in the afternoon sun, his ears bouncing like Bo Derek's braids. In those final moments, his magnificence seemed to drift in slow motion like an errant balloon from Macy's Parade. I imagine myself a matador, clutching red silk instead of a small rug, turning, arching my back, sucking it in as he sweeps past. Whoosh! But Mack turns on

a dime. *Puppies* can do this, and his head, the size and shape of a Blue Hubbard squash, nuzzles me thoroughly, at this moment an exhilarating memory relished from a Pittsburg, NH porch, and a sequence sure to repeat itself when this journey ends.

Two nights will be spent here at the Spruce Cone Lodge. My two bedroom knotty pine suite includes a combination kitchen/dining/living room, small bath and shower, extra blankets piled on the bed, and a small TV. The North Country is still very cool. Snow is seen in low-lying patches along the road. The folks downstate wouldn't be wearing shorts and tees as they were this morning, not in these parts. Early on, it was decided that much of this journey would be spontaneous, except for a couple of advance reservations. The visit to Graceland and a place to stay in Memphis on the nineteenth anniversary of Elvis's passing needed to be assured, so I called Motel 6 in West Memphis, Arkansas for the 16th of August. Also, and because this would be my first stop, I felt the need to reserve a room up here in the cork—plan ahead whether you need to or not. Memorial Day weekend is over, however, and the fishing crowd has left, so all is quiet and still pretty much off-season. Quiet that is, but for *Smiley* out here on the porch.

Soon I'll head for the border in search of moose, the ones that hang out along the highway waiting for humans with cameras, the one on my itinerary.

Signed, *Flirts with Dogs*

Pittsburg: "The Moose at Dusk Await."

Creating a soundtrack to this odyssey was a good idea, certain pieces to trigger memories later on in *The Home*. So it begins, according to the first line of my itinerary: "Memorial Day, Concord to Pittsburg, the moose at dusk await." The synthesized music of Ray Lynch serenades my drive up Route 3, weaving north to Quebec. Tantalizing signals are offered along the road: *Brake for moose—it could save your life! Moose crossing—next 19 miles*

Driving slowly past First and Second Connecticut Lakes in late afternoon, ever northward to Third Connecticut Lake. I've run out of America. No moose. Turn south, cruise the strip again, more slowly this time, look carefully. There can't **not** be moose! They call it "Moose Alley." C'mon! The itinerary said!

He was browsing a roadside bog in gold light, *Itinerary-Moose*, lifting his head to showcase his rack. He stopped chewing to study my car, suddenly parked at the opposite side of the road. Yess! I turned up the volume as the music played, New Age harpsichord, a fitting mood, magnifying the glorious power of the lowering sun against forest green and the deep brown coat of *I-Moose*. I replayed the tape, watching him watch my camera, breathing a thank you to *Master Weaver* as our agenda played through chapter one. He turned and ambled slowly backstage, stepping out of the dream, stopping a couple of times to look my way.

Well of course he'd be there! It's out of my hands now, as I've said all along. And *I-Bison* waits for its close-up in Dakota.

Signed, *Destiny Riding*

Arose at 5:00 a.m. Tuesday for another hunt, and they, along with a number of deer appeared in sporadic mirage along the road, surreal and quiet in the absence of traffic, my rearview mirror reflecting the overcast as a duck skims the flat muted slate of First Connecticut Lake.

I stopped for coffee back at the lodge with a couple of hangers-on from the fishing weekend. The wood panel walls are papered with maps and charts, antlers, hornet nests, bird nests, and more than a few preserved mammals staring blankly from the opposite wall. The owners knew Jim back in the old days down in Pittsfield, and Gary's eyes seemed to glass over when I filled him in on the journey ahead, as if a lifelong yearning had suddenly surfaced. "Been up here thirteen years now, a lot to leave at this point...too late to start over...but I'd love to do what you're doing." "I'd do it in a heartbeat!" stated his wife Doris. The power of her voice seemed to slice the air, breaking a conversational spell. "Up here it's ten months of winter and two months of poor sleddin'!"

A tall, lanky man resembling Peter O'Toole in work clothes ambled into the room and poured a cup of coffee. He was there to mow the grounds. Sixty-five, I learned later when he spoke of his approaching retirement, of dwindling benefits and his military service in Korea and Vietnam, a sad looking man. Said he planned to go to *The Wall* himself this summer "if things work out." He did brighten when moose were discussed. Said he'd been following the twins, a pair of yearlings, guessing that the mother, about to calf again, had sent them packing. "Saw 'em this mornin' wanderin' the clearin' up by Otter Hollow, out on their own, looked a little dazed." I spotted him later, *mountain man*, mowing the fields. No wave, though. Over and over the words of Joseph Conrad: "We live as we dream, alone."

French Speak on the radio up here, inflection universal. Straight news easy, occasional reports from foreign correspondents, static out of Israel, then a change in tone for a commercial, the voice more animated, followed by the weather and entertainment news: "Gladeeess Knight avec les Pipps, oui!"

Picked up a rock for Joey's cross country collection at the shore of Third Connecticut Lake, Rhode Island Joey, age ten, blond, Huck Finn or Bart Simpson, a smidge of each. Here's rock #1 all the way from the Granite State. Some distant echoes from a few honking crows, otherwise a contemplative silence here at the still waters, Canada's border a quiet place.

Later Tuesday: joy and pain, a thin veil separates them. Phoning home to my daughter should hold such joy on these thrilling days of liftoff. Why does it hurt so, a gulp away from tears. This is going to hurt. I must toughen myself to that ache. And why is Golda Meow growling at people? She doesn't do that! Grumpy old cat. *By the time she adjusts, Yogi, she'll have to readjust all over again. Tell me this is worth it, Wilfred. What's driving this?*

Back on the road at dusk, an old hand now at cruising Moose Alley, a busy place if you pick the right hour in downtown wilderness. The young ones are curious. One pair came within feet of my car, demonstrating a most ungainly appearance in their shabby spring suits, reminding me at once of the adorable mooseling blocking traffic in front of my house. They appear to move with a certain grace, as if rising above the tattered clothes and long ears. Squint your eyes, and it might be a mutant deer, maybe the head of a kangaroo, or an oversized jackrabbit, but with the wrong legs, an unfinished moose-in-progress. The decision to exit seems made abruptly, a quick sideward glance, nose in the air, leaving for parts unknown in elegant stride. But that bull! The one at sunset, *I-Moose* stopping in full frame to look my way, his broad velvet nose at a standstill. *God's great piece a work,* I whispered.

Following a perfect nap this afternoon, the first real sleep in a month of preparing for liftoff, a turkey grinder with red wine proved sumptuous in my north woods room of knotty pine.

Quote of the Day: *"Ten months of winter, two months of poor sleddin'!"*—Doris Bedell

Wednesday, May 29

It was snowing in Pittsburg this morning as coffee was shared at the Lodge with Gary, Doris and mountain man of few words, the man who'd like to talk some more about Richard Bishop on *The Wall*, who "couldn't make E-8 back in Hawaii, so signed on for 'Nam back in sixty-four and died twenty-eight days after he got there." This was revealed as I prepared to leave and asked if there was anyone I could give a nod to on his behalf. He sat slumped on the sofa, his head hinged toward the floor, lifting his hand with a slight wave. "Hope to get down there this summer myself. Have a safe trip," said Mr. O'Toole.

Ray Lynch's *Pastorale* serenaded its way along the curves, as if riding a wave sideways, hangin' ten along the Connecticut River, blurred streaks of dandelions alongside. Stopped for breakfast at the Wilderness Restaurant down in Colebrook where the waitress resembled an old friend who had left this hole in the wall years ago and moved to Florida. In calico blue and high-heeled shoes, she owned a room, not to mention its dance floor, but could run a chain saw "no problem!" She was the "Big-Boned Gal" straight out of kd lang's tune, and over at the Quik-Mart, there was another one—Colebrook's clones: blond, big boobs, tiny waist, high cheek bones, perfect teeth—all us "losers" hated 'em in high school.

I was half-reading *USA Today*, listening to the clone as she catered with practiced skill to all the seventy somethings, grumpy ol' fellas assessing the political scene, belly laughs, sentences ending in *gate*…"Big govament, damn politicians…head up their ass…greedy bastids!" Above all the chatter, as if shouting from the page before me, another *Siren* from outer space inserted itself to my ongoing trek: "Elvis in Cleveland, San Jose Ballet, Blue Suede Shoes!"

CHAPTER 15

Vermont

Sittin' on the dock of this bay in Newport, Vermont, waiting for one-hour photo processing, many *mooses* materializing. I would call this Newport, RI with elbow room. A freight train creeps through town. Its chugging echoes across Lake Memphremagog that mirrors the mountains in grey blue lines against the sky. (According to a horse's mouth, here's how it's said: memfra-MAY-gog.) The whistle's high-pitched howl fades on this cool, bright morning as I bask in the sun on a wharf hemmed with sailboats. City sounds from the main street trickle down the hill in muted intermittent chatter, while gulls trade gibberish at the corner of the dock and a golden retriever interrupts the water at a nearby landing, over and over after a red ball. Two men march past me in steady tread, balancing the weight of a large mast, conversation brisk, headed for a starting gate, ready to burst, the day is theirs. Soothing and calm, this lounge in the sun, virtual peace shouldn't be rushed. Come August, in the heat of Memphis I shall wish for the fresh cool of this air and the blue-on-blue aura of the harbor. Oh, and that freight train whispering its refrain across the lake, propelling me outward, rocket booster to outer space.

From here to my brother's ten-room doghouse and a visit with my niece Lauryn who probably won't absorb who "*Ant* Gloria" really is. Would I be the half-*ant*, her father being my half-brother? Steve and Judy came along after the war, after Wilfred's second marriage, while I remained with his sister Arlene who raised me thereafter in small town, rural Rhode Island—family proximity, back and forth between homes, part-time siblings, vacation trips here and there, birthdays, graduations, Judy five years younger than I, and Steve ten years younger than she. He and his wife Patty moved up here, living rent-free in a dilapidated farmhouse for ten years, daylight through the cracks, bottomless woodstove in winter, working nonstop, saving to build the mountaintop manse in which they and many pets now reside.

Thursday, May 30, Green-Green, it's Green I Say!

Northern Vermont oozes green smattered with lighter and darker shades of green and dandelion gold, spring at its pinnacle. Enya serenades the meandering road, so many random thoughts, like Golda Meow, wondering how she's adapting to city life. This must be how Manhattan once appeared, giant quadrants, squares of pasture on a rural *Monopoly* board, here a white farm, next a red one, barns, towering silos, cattle drifting past the window across Vermont's green miles. Damn! Didn't I just use the bathroom back there in Newport? "We'll be at your brother's soon," Wilfred whispered. Right. Think of other things—never seen so many dandelions in one space! Dandelions bring to mind my grandmother's outhouse of yore, a two-holer, I believe.

The Hathaway mountain homestead, three miles up a dirt road, is located outside Montgomery Center, fifteen miles from the Canadian border. It houses five dogs and an assortment of cautious cats that reside upstairs, thanks to a vigilant German shepherd, ironically named Buddy. There's also a horse and a pony in the barn; oh, and the humans, Steve, Patty, and Lauryn, age eight, who was scheduled to play softball on this day. Her father, the coach, stood surrounded in the late afternoon sun, a human beehive valiantly managing the clamor of his second grade swarm, all voicing a choice of position because "she played it last week." Following a progression of spirited debates as to who would play which, harmony was restored, Lauryn not yet in tune with certain protocol: "When we're on the field, I'm not Dad...you're part of the team...no whining about position!" *Three-strikes-you're-out* is not the rule here. This being a *learning experience,* it was at-bat until one was hit, so innings grew longer in proportion to the lowering sun. PS: Coach Hathaway is a great dad!

This country is still trying to decide which Memorial Day should be celebrated. Memorial Day observed, according to the calendar, is the last Monday in May. But this Thursday, May 30, is Memorial Day in Enosburg Falls, Vermont as the parade marches through town, Lauryn among the Brownie Scouts. Brisk spring weather blusters across the green with rolling gray clouds and punishing bursts of wind. Veterans carry colors that snap and *Taps* is played. A Vietnam vet offers the address, reminding me of *Mountain Man* back in Pittsburg and his old friend, the late Richard Bishop.

CHAPTER 16

New York

Leave New England

Spring weather continued its rant, too much so for a stomach-friendly cruise across Lake Champlain, so I decided against the ferry and headed north for the Bridge to New York. A small herd of Highlander cattle stood by a gate at the road's edge, a stunning committee of shaggy strawberry blondes. Turning right could bring me to Quebec just inches away, but turning left was final thrust via I-87, New England left behind along the Adirondack Highway, headed for Cooperstown and a nod to Cousin Wilma at the Baseball Hall of Fame.

Settling in for the night, unpacking the car, would become routine: find lodging, learn its price via bag phone, fill out the guest card, unpack the car—camera bag, small overnight bag, word processor, and file box. The Fran Cove Motel in Lake George sits on a hill among other such lodgings boasting AAA, swimming pool, and cable TV. But this one isn't in Pittsburg, just up the road, no longer in New England, no turning back. Took a short drive down to the Main Street and had dinner in a small café, aware of second looks, she's-alone-looks, real or imagined—antipasto, red wine, and lentil soup.

Hindsight: Next time, scope out side street eateries. HellOOoo! Main Street, resort town, Memorial Day weekend!

"Welcome to Lake George Village Our Meter Enforcement Officer has issued you a Courtesy Violation Notice. They will be returning. Enjoy yourself in our Community. We apologize for having to enforce our meters because of limited parking. Please respect our parking regulations, and we hope you return soon."

—Mayor, Village of Lake George

*****

Rah Rah Wilma!

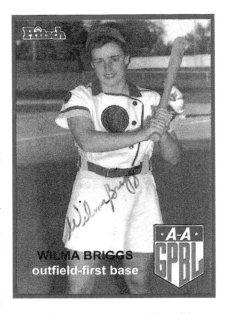

WILMA BRIGGS
outfield-first base

In 1992 when Tom Hanks gained weight and an Oscar nomination for Penny Marshall's film *A League of Their Own*, I learned an interesting bit of family history as it connects to the All-American Girls' Baseball League during World War II.

Wilma Briggs is a retired school teacher, and at the Hathaway family reunion that summer, with first, second, and third generations grouped separately for various photos, I was able to place seldom seen relatives into better context. She is my father's first cousin, blonde, trim, youthful, unmistakably athletic, twenty years older than I, but would I ever think of trying a game of tennis with her?

It wasn't the usual how-long-has-it-been chats causing a stir that day. Sure, the Hathaways were proud of Wilma, but in 1992, most Rhode Islanders had become aware of Wilma "Briggsie" Briggs, the baseball star.

The backyard of her family's dairy farm in East Greenwich, RI is where she learned to play the game from her father, a baseball nut who even named one of his sons for Jimmie Foxx. He coached a local team known as the Frenchtown Farmers, and, long story short, in a family that included seven brothers and four sisters, Wilma's birth coming in the midst of the brothers, she did what they did. If she could do the barn work with them, she could play ball, and she did it well. Starting high school in 1944, she was already an accomplished basketball player and gymnast, and her coach who also played for her father's team asked her to play first base that summer. In her senior year of high school she played baseball on the boys' team.

Soon after high school graduation in 1948, she went to Fort Wayne, Indiana, to try out for the All-American Girls' Baseball League. She was playing right outfield by her second week with the Ft. Wayne Daisies, and in her first year the team made it to the play-offs, losing eventually to the Rockford Peaches (Gena Davis's team in the movie). *Briggsie* led the Daisies to three league pennants. She was the second all-time leader in home runs in 1953, and when the league ended in 1954 she continued playing softball for local teams.

In 1965 at age thirty-five she went to college, and for the next twenty-three years taught elementary school. It's well known that during recess, Wilma played baseball with about sixty youngsters "to stay in shape," for local softball teams. Her baseball career ended in 1992 after the release of *A League of Their Own* where she appeared with former teammates during the film's final credits, and soon after, became Rhode Island's foremost, autograph-signing, face-in-the-papers celebrity, and a huge hit at the Hathaway Family Reunion.

High Fly into Cooperstown

Found Wilma's name on a plaque at the Hall of Fame and lingered for a while. Thanks to Ken Burns' *Baseball*, I'm at least a bit more informed in the sport, even beyond some of the big names like Babe Ruth or Micky Mantle whose locker is here at the Hall. I might even come through a general baseball category in *Jeopardy*. But I'm sounding like an empty head, one who knows next to nothing about the sport. Wilma would be so disappointed. What is it though, about Ted Williams? Images of that swing, his grace and power, signing up for the war at the peak of his career. I'm in love with the imagery, over and over that swing. If only I liked baseball.

Classic Yogi: "If people don't want to come out to the ballpark, how are you going to stop them?"

*****

Friday, May 31
The Colonial Motel, Skaneateles, NY—$45.36

Magnificent Saturday morning here among the Finger Lakes at the tip of Lake Skaneateles (*skanny-ATLAS*), Iroquois meaning *long lake*. An endless green meadow sprawls across the highway from my bench in the sun. Breakfast is free as I savor strong black coffee, strawberries, cantaloupe, and a fresh blueberry muffin. Lovin' New York in June!

"You're in luck," said the desk clerk. "This is our last weekend of off-season rates, a deal at forty-five dollars! Forty-five dollars? It's got to get better than this. Leaving for Buffalo, 9:30 a.m.

Niagara Falls

It's a fact that Niagara Falls is a long drive from the Finger Lakes, and I sit, not behind the wheel at last, on another bench in the sun. Tourist season is not yet in full swing, so it's relatively quiet here on the American side. Couples stroll the walkways as Niagara pounds its hypnotic roar, the force most definitely with me. A special postcard wants to be written from such a romantic place, and to just the right person who comes playfully to mind: "Dumped in New Hampshire," a formerly wealthy divorcee whose marriage, all those wonderful years together, was terminated abruptly by a philandering husband who needed space. But this Lord & Taylor lady, the queen of *sardonica*, has maintained her sense of humor—along with the great clothes—and has fine-tuned at least a scad of *men-are-pigs* one-liners.

Yo, *Dumped!*

Having the best time here in Niagara. Oops, forgot a husband.

Ray Cutler: Why don't you ever get a dress like that?
Polly Cutler: Listen. For a dress like that, you've got to start laying plans when you're about thirteen.

—*Niagara,* 1953, starring Marilyn
Monroe and Joseph Cotton

CHAPTER 17

The Cleveland Approach

Saturday, June 1
The Miracle Motel, East Springfield, Pa.—$31.80

What was that about my plan to average sixty to one hundred miles a day? Drove way too long today, ending up here at the Miracle Motel in the northwest corner of Pennsylvania. *NYPD Blue* character, Sipowicz, might refer to it glibly as *some fleabag outside Erie*, a trailer-style strip of rooms located near a large farmhouse, surrounded by lawn, two large shade trees included. What this is, is an oven just off the interstate chosen mostly out of exhaustion following a quick rate request back at "***Econo**-Lodge: Check out our lower rates.*" Straight-faced, spoke the desk clerk: $109, plus tax, per person, per night!

Strategy is set now for the Cleveland approach. Just get me through this financial maze. The Rock & Roll Hall of Fame was the main reason for Cleveland, but now a ballet commemorating the life of Elvis. "Blue Suede Shoes" holds its premier at the Cleveland State Theatre. Irresistible!

And it's a *miracle!* This rickety air conditioner works after all as my boxcar accommodation begins to cool down, that and a bed too. Life on the road is a wonder.

Signed, *Trailer Trash*

PS: Sleeping tight with pepper spray

SERIOUS PROTECTION AGAINST CRIME

Pepper Spray - A Red Pepper Personal Defense Weapon

For this product to be fully effective, you must engulf the assailant's face, especially the eyes, nose, and mouth. This product generally has a range of up to ten to twelve feet. Wind and other conditions may alter the range or effectiveness. Shield your eyes and face if you must fire into the wind; however, avoid spraying into the wind if possible.

- Unlock the red actuator lever by moving the lever to the right;
- Aim at face of assailant;
- Press down firmly, using short bursts.

CHAPTER 18

Ohio

Sunday, June 2 and 3
Motel 6, Middleburg Heights, OH—$86.98

Interesting encounters today while wandering the byways of Cleveland. I was browsing for a snack when the Sunoco comedian shouted across the store, "Sorry, your credit card's denied!" I looked up in horror. This trek has barely begun, what does *that* mean! "Just kidding." He grinned. It could take months to get that going with a total stranger back in New England. And the women with their umbrellas headed for the theater downtown who invited me to get out of the rain, a common thread with folks along the way, questions about this journey; they would love to do the same. It stokes the passion and carries me through the *fleabags* and down times.

It was time to eat a decent meal so at *Friendlies* when I ordered sides of rice, four-bean salad, and green salad as well, the waitress had to ask what I was going for...avoiding the usual offerings an attention getter.

Talked with Michele earlier. Cranky cat still foiling Delilah's play plans.

I was really counting on a good night's sleep, but it ain't gonna happen tonight. Not after this day. It was that random pickup back there in Colebrook, NH, when fate handed me a copy of *USA Today* with its summons to the Cleveland State Theatre for the premiere of "Blue Suede Shoes." Ballet will never be the same! The show is going on tour throughout the year, ending in Memphis next summer marking the twentieth anniversary of *The King's* passing.

It is danced to remastered recordings of his music, "Guitar Man," the overture, vibrating throughout the auditorium as if Elvis himself were singing, like the *Phantom of the Opera* from an unseen balcony. With costumes and sets by fashion designer Bob Mackie, the stage is framed by giant legs straddling a guitar in broad neon strokes of paint against black velvet, one knee twisted to the side in mid swing. As the giant guitar rises, music and dance weave the lullaby of early rock and roll: a prom queen, a not-so-prom-queen, a greaser—*Happy Days* in ballet shoes, our fifties high school the setting.

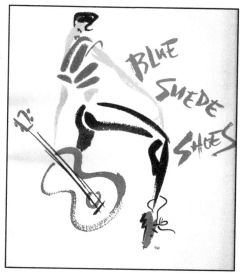

The second act opens with GI Blues, the army, and sweethearts back home. One character, a soldier in white light, dances on an empty stage, *Are You Lonesome Tonight? In the Ghetto* follows in the opposite wing, dreamlike, performed with sad, haunting perfection. Technology—the old 45s never sounded this good, an exquisite baritone. Don't let it be forgot. The man could sing! When this one hits the fan, Yogi, there'll be another comeback all over again.

Monday, June 3

The lady at Motel 6 issued precise directions: take the East 9th Street exit all the way to the Lake. "When you pass the ball field, you're right on, a straight shot." Great going if you pay attention. But no! Take the wrong exit. Warning, warning! NH car going wrong way on a one way, everyone blow your horn!

Oh well, all's well after it ends. Never did notice a ball field, but when direction had been found to *the lake*, I nodded heavenward to my late brother-in-law, the only one who'd have the perfect line for such a moment. He's out there doing cosmic standup with things like, "Maybe that big black arrow confused her...probably thought it meant *One-Way, Ohio Cars Only...*" *ba-da-boom—ting-ing-ing* I blame it on Bob Seger, exquisitely loud in my cool Geo, Cleveland's skyline before me, bound for the Rock and Roll Hall of Fame...*Just take those old records off the shelf...today's music ain't got the same soul... oh, what was the arrow?*

Welcome to the Rock & Roll Hall of Fame and Museum, Now Get Lost!

A shining glass pyramid sits on the shore of Lake Erie, and on climbing the steps to its acre-wide cement lawn, I was pulled to the music, a kid again, entranced by an unseen cool Pied Piper. Rock and roll rises like steam from its crystal peak as Mick Jagger sets the mood. Oh to dance, but it's early morning, I'm alone in a parking lot and I'm not my brassy sister.

The basement is filled with mannequins, legends congregated forever in their cool period threads: The Supremes, Alice Cooper, Elton John, Elvis, his *Comeback Special* clothes on loan from Priscilla. Constant rhythms pulsate from video cubes tucked in random corners, floor-to-ceiling movie montages of the history, the early years, of Hank Williams, Robert Johnson, Howlin' Wolf, Bessie Smith and Lead Belly. Freight trains belching through southern towns in grainy black and white, folks along the tracks, singing, dancing, a wailing genre hurtling through Memphis toward the Big Bang as Tupelo's child explodes across the decades. Time seemed to step aside. I've been here since morning, and it's nearly five, wallowing teen angel, hangin' out again at Vern's Diner, Quonset Point RI, *Stardate 1956*, dancing to Little Richard, Elvis and Chuck Berry. Murray the K, *WINS, WINS, WINS, NY!* Did ya see him on Ed Sullivan? Only showed his top half!

Then came the brown paper bag under glass, scrawled with faded pencil, John Lennon's melody singing itself through my brain: "*There are places…I remember…some have gone…and some remain…*"

At the summit of I. M. Pei's crystal pyramid, Lake Erie fades to the horizon like the Atlantic back home, and the words of Pink Floyd push from *the wall:* "Accept the burden of insight…take the road less traveled…embark on the often painful journey…"—Roger Waters, 1995

Back at Motel 6 a lonesome dog wails from a neighboring room, pitiful whines that in any other setting would cause me distress, but held in the aura of Cleveland's pyramid, the hound's despair echoes in a bluesy howl—enchanting, the timeless anguish of Howlin' Wolf.

Dear Mr. Pei: Your Cleveland pyramid is way cooler than that other one in Paris. And my name is *GLORRRRRReeee-uh!* G-L-O-R-I-Aeeee *GLORRRRRReeee-uh!*

Kent, Ohio, Tuesday, June 4

In the highway lottery I hit a sort of *trifecta* today: Quik-Lube, one-hour photo, and laundry in the same plaza. ATM annoying, however: "Sorry, this machine cannot process this request." And speaking of high finance, I'm an old hand now at dining along the shoestring: Breakfast at Friendlee's (take-out, no tip): bagel, juice, coffee, $2.50; Lunch, Wendy's salad bar: $1.99; Dinner, Friendlies **à la carte**: four-bean salad, rice, garden salad with tip: $6.00. Total food: $10.49.

Initially, Ohio was going to be a quick pass, except for the Hall of Fame, but then came *Blue Suede Shoes* and now a quick visit with my long-ago brother-in-law and his wife who live in Kent with their Himalayan cat, which by the way, could have inspired Paula

Poundstone's classic line: "The problem with cats is they get the exact same look on their face, whether they see a moth or an ax murderer."

I was dating Roger's big brother Mike back in the sixties, the boy next door and the father of our future children, when in February '64, Roger asked a question for the ages: "Are you watching tonight? The Beatles on Ed Sullivan!" In the glorious decade to follow, of bad hair and leisure suits, he and his first wife were seventies *American Gothic,* straight out of Woodstock. They were wed in New Hampshire on a hill at sunset overlooking Lily Pond, he draped in polyester, she in a peasant dress, her long straight hair, sixties classic, was parted in the center, crowned with a circle of white flowers. Paul Stookey's choirboy voice crooned his *Wedding Song* from a tape deck, "There is Love."

We planted and harvested our food, baked bread with whole grains, and read the gospel of nutrition according to Adele Davis, organic this and herbal that, the importance of vitamin A and organ meats. Niki and I were wannabe artists, she a free spirit, more skilled in the process than I. In hindsight, she was more Madonna before her time, too *far out* for a marriage made in heaven. It was no longer happening, and after several years and two sons, it played itself out when she packed the car and drove away as Roger watched her car, their marriage, fade in the distance. He wore a look of sadness I can't forget.

On his Wednesday off, we toured Kent State's memorial to the slain kids and the hillside planted with as many daffodils as those who died in Vietnam. Akron was next, home of the Soap Box Derby, struggling for preservation, for renewal, its bleachers in need of repair and the garage running out of space for its collection of vintage cars dating back to the thirties. A perfect, well, *vehicle,* I think, for Bart Simpson, America's derring-do poster kid surfing the great hill. Memo to Fox: How about a shot in the arm for Akron's slope? A fast poster graphic springs to mind of Bart the Bold, or how about Lisa going with gravity at the wheel of her intelligently designed crate, bejeweled with tiny saxophones honoring Bleeding Gums Murphy.

A cavernous dome sits nearby in a flat, expansive field. It's used for blimp building, and alone there in its space looks like a colossal, grimy termite queen.

North to Michigan
Thursday, June 6

Back on the road, headed for Michigan, I followed a dump truck for miles in a long line of traffic and nearly followed it off the highway into a construction area, hardhats shaking back and forth, eyes rolling most likely; one of them was smiling, though. And it wasn't 'til much later that I noticed Roger's additions to my vehicle: decals, smiling red Cleveland Indians, *those* Indians, **that** ball field!

CHAPTER 19

Michigan

Mucky Bottom Manor in Milford, Michigan, is the home of Suzanne Hasque, artist extraordinaire, who breezed into a Florida room four years ago when thoughts of this journey first began to stir. We were guests at Wendy's wedding, and in five minutes flat it was clear that we'd met somewhere in another life. So we made a date for today's meeting: "When, not if, you come through Michigan, stop in Milford," she instructed, "Not *if*, but *when*! This journey must be taken!"

First a tour of the neighborhood in her golf cart across a lawn that surrounds a small pond. A towering dead tree stood before us, the object of contention between Suzanne and her other half who'd like to have at it with a chain saw, while she views such things as grand sculpture, its arms extended in perfect symmetry, straight and proud, an extraordinary arboreal mummy. It would seem we were miles from civilization, but as the crow flies, one of Ford's largest assembly plants lies two miles to the east, an island in a sea of white Lincolns.

Continuing through the neighbor's barnyard, we were noticed by all but one of its many Morgans, the horse unaccustomed to fencing and so roamed freely about, too busy trimming the landscape to even lift its head. We drove through the barn, an intoxicating aroma from my perspective, communing with the new moms and curious foals stretching forward to greet.

The walk through her house offered paintings and pottery at every turn, then her studio, and after that her husband's study, or so she says, but many of her projects have claimed the space. Several of her paintings were done in France, all of them enhanced here by the exquisite layout of her home, the grand finale being her paisley bathroom of saturated reds, known by her as the *hormone room*. A spectacular painting hangs above the porcelain throne, *Woman with Poppies* whose face echoes the many self-portraits of Frida Kahlo. She is draped in velvet, cobalt blue trimmed with gold, a large poppy tucked behind her ear against ebony curls that drop to a bare shoulder, arms laden with crimson blooms.

A quick lunch and I was back on the road.

Thursday, June 6
Motel 6, Flint, Michigan—$35.46

If Michigan's a mitten (right hand, palm up) then my home tonight in Motel 6 is located mid thumb here in Flint. Next stop, Mackinaw City to the north and tomorrow's much anticipated crossing of the great bridge. Homework warned me that it happens sometimes two or three times a day, mostly in the fall of the year when someone wants to reach Michigan's *Upper Peninsula* but can't face the five mile drive across the Mackinac Bridge, among the world's longest spans rising two hundred feet above the straits. Two words: panic attack. Drivers come to a halt, while a professional bridge-crosser slips behind the wheel, a free escort provided by the bridge authority. This bit of history served to heighten my anticipation, such as the unfortunate woman driving a Yugo, a subcompact blown over the northbound side, dropping into the strait. *Sub*compact, indeed!

All-you-can-eat salad at Wendy's, tall ice water, no tip, total dinner: $3.17. Remembering "Mountain Man" back in Pittsburg. Sad man. I shall send him a Wall rubbing of Richard Bishop's name

75

from 1964, the long-ago conflict that seems to pull at me in unexpected twinges.

> *Quote of the Week:* 75 North: Prison Area Do Not
> Pick Up Hitchhikers

> Signed, *Forewarned in Flint*

Friday, June 7
Anchors Inn, Mackinaw City, Michigan—$42.12

Time-Out!

It's a fact in Michigan that whichever way you see it spelled—ac or aw—as in Mackinaw City, Mackinac Island, or the mighty Mackinac Bridge, it's always pronounced Macki**NAW**. It's a part of history, *Michinnimakinong* the original Indian word. Then the French arrived from the north in 1715, and after that the British came from the south and defeated the French. Language evolves already! Don't embarrass yourself in Michigan by uttering the word MackiNACK. It's pronounced NAW. Macki*NAW*. Don't make them say it again!

Enjoyed a picnic lunch this afternoon on the shore of Lake Huron and soon imagined myself a player in Hitchcock's movie. Who hasn't seen at least a few scenes of *The Birds,* its menace springing to mind when more than ten or twelve feathered suits gather in a nearby space. I can see her now, poor, clueless Suzanne Pleshette, seated alone on a bench next to the school, unaware, as one black bird alights on the jungle gym behind her, then another, then some fifty more.

I chose a picnic table at the crest of a lovely slope where pathways meander to the shore below. The entrance to the bridge, tomorrow's crossing, waits across the lawn to my left, while the great span stretches beyond to the Upper Peninsula, its far end gauzed in fog as the twin towers beckon, an awesome *Mackinaw* moment. I was about to dine on fried chicken when the first gull lowered itself to the lawn nearby, then one or two more, seven, then eight. The first gull, a gull boss, began to posture if another got too close to the table, to *my* meal. His wings flapped vigorously, raising him *accidentally* to the opposite bench, his head eye level with my Styrofoam dinnerware. He glanced quickly in my direction, then tipped his head at my food, took a couple of sidesteps, probably checking for sub-gulls, then a couple of steps back, in side-togethers, like learning the foxtrot back in grade school. Now and then he'd cock his head to the side as if to question *my* rude behavior, reminding me of Golda-back-home sitting in for a snack, her orange face feigning politeness. Two couples walking the path stopped short to look, but eight or ten gulls were not going to mess with my Michigan mood. I turned to them with a quick smile, startled by the thirty or forty gulls standing in silent vigil at my back. Quote of the day hard to come up with at this moment. I turned back to my gull companion, catching his rude thoughts: *Are you gonna eat all that, lady?*

On a tip from one of the natives back at the motel, the one who firmly explained the correct pronunciation of *MackiNAW,* I returned to the slope at sunset for a splendid grand finale—a deepening orange sky and bridge lights that twinkled like stars in a pathway across the lakes, Huron rippling softly at my feet, inviting meditation, quiet history whispering to the sand. In the absence of a tripod I set the camera on a picnic table and held the shutter open a few seconds, hoping for the best.

*Saturday, June 8*th
The Vagabond Motel, Paradise, Michigan—$32.70

Navigating the great bridge this morning was a magnificent sail to the sky, sunlight broadcasting its charm across the water to Mackinac Island. The daunting specter of the unfortunate Yugo was forgotten as I drifted through Michigan's back door, carried to the sky with "Exile," Enya's enchanting choir of Indian pipes.

Accommodations here in paradise are plain and simple, home-like and cozy, as in knotty pine and quilts, a welcoming address among the trees. Idyllic reruns cross my mind, of the bridge, the anticipation, the distance covered to now, the itinerary, the drive from New England to this long-planned destination, a seemingly tranquil pond that simply sweeps along a quiet road to Whitefish Point. The big lake shimmered orange in the lowering sun, like hammered copper, the only traffic a family of Canada Geese at the rocky shore where I found a stone for Joey's collection. It was ceremoniously plucked from the water, safely stashed in its own baggie: *Michigan/ Lake Superior*—surely a prize-winning *show and tell.*

Sunday, June 9th

The Shipwreck Museum at Whitefish Point is a white clapboard building with a red roof. Double doors open to a small foyer where the price of admission is paid and heavy glass doors must then be pushed with some effort into the next room, resisting, as if straining against a wall of water, the perfect sensation for what is to come. Darkness at the bottom of the lake, but for the wall panels, each one offered in spotlight. It's a bizarre promenade beneath the sea, escorted to the crawl of a somber *New Age* melody, the ghostly dirge pulling like undertow into the deep, oozing dread as the walls tell stories of the big lake they call *Gitchigoomi.* Brass bells and diving helmets play with refracted light as each panel recalls the history of Superior's angry gales, *the Witch of November,* of doomed souls entombed in its icy water. Life-size divers hover, suspended from the blackness overhead, while a scale replica of the Edmund Fitzgerald takes up its corner of the deep, the ship that lies broken in two at the bottom of the Lake—729 feet long, 13,632 gross tons. This pace, the lingering dark melody is perfect theater, a mesmerizing passage. The sporadic murmur of gulls and distant foghorns is barely realized, but seems to commandeer the psyche in an oddly engaging nightmare of rolling waves that engulf and release, like black rippling gauze, panel to panel, rusted anchors, ships' wheels, another panel, another awful tale, to the door—daylight, so soon.

Beyond the museum, the lighthouse and a nearly deserted beach invites further steps beyond, infinite grassy dunes and a shore lined with speckled stones worn smooth like Fabergé eggs. A graveyard of driftwood scatters the beach for miles, whole trees bleached pale gray. The gentle surf of Lake Superior covers my feet, sloshing a bit further at intervals to soak the hem of my jeans, not as cold as expected. Across the horizon, a freighter moves in silent passage from the Soo locks out of Sault Ste. Marie. Walkman in place, cue Mr. Lightfoot: *The Wreck of the Edmund Fitzgerald*, an early thread woven to the *Vagabond* soundtrack: Tranquility beach here, Gloria Jean has landed!

> ***Quote of the Day:*** *"Ships at a distance have every man's wish on board. For some they come in with the tide. For others they sail forever on the horizon, never out of sight, never landing until the watcher turns his eyes away in resignation, his dreams mocked to death by time. That is the life of man."*
>
> —Zora Neale Hurston, "Their Eyes Were Watching God"

"Not!"

> —Gloria Jean, "Vagabond Chic"

A bird sanctuary near the museum offers Adirondack chairs and a blissful, middle-of-nowhere stretch in the sun. Birds A to Z flutter in droves at crate-size feeders—Blue Jays, grosbeaks, finches, black-capped chickadees, too many to count. Spaghetti supper at a local inn. Duluth, Minnesota tomorrow by way of Wisconsin's forehead.

Signed, *"Lady of the Lakes"*

Monday, June 10
The Crestview Motel, Ironwood, Michigan—$25.60

From Paradise to Ironwood, crossing Michigan's upper peninsula through Hiawatha National Forest is a highway for dreamers. Wetlands twinkle with sunlight, and streams vanish in never-ending byways to the blue sky beyond, fields of dandelions, quilts of yellow and green, hemmed by a railway, Lake Superior's expanse to the north. Awareness of time blurs, trancelike, now and then a town, filling station, store, motel and bar—always a bar. In the town of Munising (MEWN-a-sing) where the highway sweeps around a horseshoe cove, I came upon a medley of diminished icebergs parked in flat water, a silent herd of porous white shapes run aground. This prompted a post card to my new friends back in Pittsburg: Gary & Doris: Greetings from the *UP*—ten months winter, two months waterskiing—maybe. Munising, Michigan, June 10.

CHAPTER 20

Minnesota

Tuesday, June 11
Moose Lake Motel, Moose Lake, Minnesota—$37.28

Moose Lake, Minnesota, south of Duluth, was a good rehearsal for the small towns to come, a total road queen, small talk with the waitress at Tootie's, turkey on whole wheat, coffee, no dessert.

Leaving the restaurant, I noticed the *Moose Lake Gazette* across the street and went in to introduce myself. In planning this journey, I had entertained the idea of seeking out a local family who might welcome my overnight stay in their barn; however, the paper's next edition was due out tomorrow, and the woman wore an all-too-familiar, *deadline-closing-in-for-God's-sake* expression, so I kept the conversation short. More farms to come along the way.

> Moose Lake Gazette—*"FARGO* 'THERE WON'T BE A BETTER FILM THAN THIS ALL YEAR!' Gene Siskel, SISKEL & EBERT
>
> —A Homespun Murder Story"

Uh…define homespun.

Wednesday, June 12
South 10th Street, Minneapolis

Graduated high school thirty-seven years ago this week. Gloria Jean, who never drove herself to Providence, today navigated the innards of Minneapolis, twice. First Cleveland and now this, another dry run for Memphis, Annapolis, the humongous *Apple* and that dawn stroll across Brooklyn's bridge. Throughout the downtown area, people lounged in the lunch-hour sun, while I, ever loyal to the path of least resistance, came upon a free parking space in front of a Vietnamese restaurant. Using chopsticks (instructions not included) #41 proved delicious.

I'm parked in front of Magenta's house on South 10th at 36th, a quiet shaded street of stucco houses, or rather, intermittently quiet, as it lies beneath the bellies-in-transit of jumbo jets headed elsewhere. She is the younger cousin I rarely see, she raised in California and I in Rhode Island, so my visit here has provided her a reason for some much needed time off. Anticipation: when did we last see each other? What does she look like? Will the time spent be awkward? I hardly know her as an adult. She's studying Art History, while my collected volumes at home include things like *Art Appreciation Made Simple* and *The Bluffer's Guide to Art, Introduced by David Frost: Know Your Jargon and Hold Your Own in Any Company*. We'll see how I keep up with the future Dr. Pierrot.

Little girl lost, my cousin Magenta, the artist formerly named Susan, doctoral candidate in Renaissance Art, "Women Painters of the Renaissance," a thesis away. Nothing happening with it now, however—divorce, caught in a financial maze, her passion on hold, trying to stay above water until the house sells. All that's left is where to go, but not one more winter in Minneapolis!

Dinner, wine, and long talks about the years between us, New England to San Diego in the sixties, both of us divorced, both of us far from home. After our late-night family history session had spent itself, I noticed a stack of volumes on the floor near my bed, one of them published in Italian. No *Bluffer's Guide* here! If time travel were a reality, I'd spin us back to Milford, Michigan, for another tour of

Suzanne's house and her *hormone* room of multiple reds, *Woman with Poppies* framed above the throne.

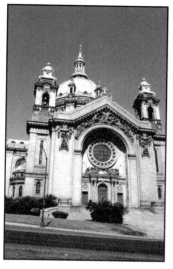

The next day we toured St. Paul, its posh Summit Avenue lined with mansions on either side, each one eclipsing the one before, not unlike Bellevue Avenue in Newport. The sun had nearly set as we rolled along the drive that overlooks the city. Then it appeared, looming overhead in fading light, beside the car, blocking all else as though it had stepped suddenly into the road, the Cathedral of St. Paul, its colossal shadow demanding awe.

Before leaving town this morning, I returned to photograph its every angle against the sky, sunlight showcasing each sculpture. From an upper colonnade, tiny tourists clustered along the aisle below appeared the size of salt shakers as janitors pushed wide mops in the glow of stained glass. I set the camera on one of the benches and held the shutter open to catch the dome overhead in natural light. One of the locals suggested I drive across town to the capitol steps for a better perspective, a full roll spent on this St. Paul address (construction began 1906, seating capacity three thousand).

June 14, 1996
Sauk Ctr., Minnesota—The Hillcrest Motel—$25.56

Sauk Center Minnesota, the birthplace of Sinclair Lewis, is located halfway between Minneapolis and Fargo/Moorhead to the north, the other twin cities. His novel, *Main Street,* was published in 1920, the story of a worldly young woman trying to change the narrow-minded nature of folks living in the American Midwest. She yearns for freedom but knows that the people of Gopher Prairie need help, and the story tells of her struggle to teach humility in this small-minded place nearly eighty years ago.

"She had found only two traditions of the American small town. The first tradition, repeated in scores of magazines every month, is that the American village remains the one sure abode of friendship, honesty, and clean sweet marriageable girls... The other tradition is that the significant features of all the villages are whiskers, iron dogs upon lawns, gold bricks, checkers, jars of gilded cattails, and shrewd comic old men who are known as 'hicks'..."

—*Main Street,* 1920, Sinclair Lewis

Gopher Prairie, its name, brings to mind the small town I'm about to see: Prairie Rose, North Dakota. Back when the itinerary was taking shape, when the map was given more scrutiny for its general routing, is when the little town called Prairie Rose was discovered in the vicinity of Fargo. So too was the town of Hathaway twenty miles west of Miles City, Montana, and the dream of finding one more insulator to place at Dad's grave when I return home—two threads woven into Rand McNally's pages along with the Cowboy Hall of Fame, Graceland, and Orient Point where Mr. Steinbeck lifted off with Charley.

Prairie Rose has little significance to my route beyond the charm of its name and my continued fantasy of that tiny town across the Mississippi. I can see its Main Street and the general store with pickle barrels and such, perhaps a dusty boardwalk with tubs of flowers. A courthouse sits at the town square and at the end of the street a small white church. It has oak pews and an antique organ with wide foot pedals, its bench topped with red-velvet cushion and above the black and white keys a medley of round knobs. In the pastures there are cows with kind faces chewing sideways while shiny backed horses drink from ponds spackled with sunlight and blackbirds sail on the breeze in graceful swoops along the fence line. It hovers across the borderline—a beguiling mirage, with more to come, as in Rosebud, Montana, where Juanita McDanold waits at the post office ten miles south of Hathaway.

CHAPTER 21

Dakota

Saturday, June 15
Motel 75, Fargo, North Dakota—$26.43

Stayed in Fargo my first night in *Dakota*—that's *west of the Mississippi*. Sipped coffee at the railroad crossing, an entertainment I plan to enjoy many times. Poked around a bookstore on Main Street and found a hardcover McMurtry: *Anything for Billy,* one of my favorites, now all the more so for its inscription: Gloria Jean, Fargo, North Dakota, June 1996. Simple gifts. Oh, and a rock for Joey from the crossing.

By the way, so much for that long-ago siren from the west, a metaphysical prank! The romance of it shone from the atlas months before—Prairie Rose under the *big sky*. As it turns out, my dream town lies to the south of Fargo, hundreds of new houses popping from the earth along tidy streets in orderly rows. You are now leaving the *Burbs.* Cue Pete Seeger…*"Little boxes on the hillside…and they all look just the same."*

Disneyworld is everywhere. The tourist center resembles a grain elevator, visually redundant one could say, but a good place to gather maps for future explorations. There's a game reserve northwest of here, and a trail through the Badlands farther west, mental pictures I now hesitate to sketch in advance.

Still enjoying thoughts of that drive through northern Minnesota, at least a couple of hours, mile after mile of space, nothing to take up the mind but blue sky, railroad crossings, grain elevators, birds sailing on the wind like kites, sun crystals across pastures and ponds, amorous cattle, shameless cattle, "…because it's June, June, June…"

Monday, June 16
Chieftain Conference Center, Carrington, North Dakota—$32.95

Drove further west to Jamestown, home of "The World's Largest Buffalo," an imposing cement sculpture, twenty-six feet tall, forty-six feet long, weighing sixty tons. Its peculiar dark hulk could be seen from the interstate nearly a mile ahead, announcing the location of the National Buffalo Museum and Frontier Village: a school, post office, and saloon; fire hall, barber shop, sheriff's office, and jail; a petting zoo of various livestock, and the Louis L'Amour Writer's Shack. This will have to do as *Prairie Rose*.

*****

Homage to Peggy Lee *(with a little help from Leiber and Stoller)*

I remember when it first hit me,
When this journey first caught fire
And the look on my face
When the lure of that prairie town
Seemed to blossom from the
map like a pop-up book

But then, months later,
parked at the street sign
I saw nothing but new
houses in tidy rows,
And I had the feeling that
something was missing,
I don't know what, but
when it was all over,
I said to myself, Is that all
there is…to Prairie Rose?

86

Is that all there is?
Is that all there is? If that's all there is, my friends…
Then let's keep driving…
If that's all…
there is…

*****

Leaving the interstate in Dakota is to be swept away, mile after mile, one pasture to the next. Cattle stand in long rows along the fence gazing quietly at the camera, attentive to my flattering chat. A small herd stood knee-deep in a pond while calves peered from beside the parent, never breaking their gaze. Red-winged and yellow-headed blackbirds plummet from fence to marsh across the straight road ahead while ducks cut trails across ponds, breaking sheets of green that coat the surface like Cling Wrap over pea soup. From Jamestown to Carrington and Devils Lake beyond, grain elevators and water tanks announce each town. This will never get old.

Welcome to Sullys Hill National Game Preserve

"Sullys Hill National Game Preserve is located on the south shore of Devils Lake, the heart of the Fort Totten Sioux Indian Reservation. Set aside in 1904 as a national park by proclamation of President Theodore Roosevelt, ten years later Congress established the big game preserve. In 1917, 15 elk arrived from Yellowstone National Park, four deer from the Fargo Agricultural Experiment Station, and six bison the next year from the Portland, Oregon City Park. It became part of the National Wildlife Refuge System in 1931, one of four refuges managed by the U.S. Fish and Wildlife service for American bison and elk."

—Visitor Center brochure,
Jamestown, ND

I followed a narrow paved road that curved through overgrown wilderness, the only human on this patch of earth able to dawdle along the way without stopping traffic, braking here and there for tardy glimpses of whatever spotted me first. Tree trunks braid themselves to the sky against thickets of green, and the marshes are dotted with water lilies that scatter the surface like tiny yellow buoys. At its outer reach lies an overlook at the crest of Sullys Hill, and getting there requires a climb, roughly a hundred wooden steps to Dakota's ceiling. Alone at the top, catching my breath was the only sound, no trucks, cars or planes, and the wonder, how many miles between me and whatever breaks the horizon. Leaving the park, I took a wrong turn and drove further into the Spirit Lake Reservation, small clusters of wood frame, one-story boxes, dreary neighborhoods, now and then a native walking the road.

Tatanka! I stopped to watch a small herd of bison munching the hillside. A couple of them stood in profile against jumbo white clouds and may have been the ones I expected to see within the reserve. Like cattle, the young ones gazed with curiosity while Pop stood closer to the fence regarding my presence, his head tilted downward a bit, as if glancing over bifocals.

On the way out of Carrington the Burlington Northern triggered the crossing bell, so I pulled over at the gate and sat on the hood of the car sipping coffee as the cars clacked in steady rhythm, a twelve-year-old again, my imaginary sister on the other fender, waving to the conductor, counting cars, waiting for the caboose. Still haven't decided which sound is more a pipeline to the soul, train whistles shouting down the tracks or foghorns across Narragansett Bay.

Listened to AM Radio along the way for local flavor, today's tunes are coming from AM KIXX, "the only station serving western Manitoba."

Tuesday, June 18
Ho Hum Motel, Minot, North Dakota—$21.55

Here in Minot I'm settled at the Ho Hum Motel. After a while you learn the names more synonymous with *reasonable*. Look for Vagabond, Sleepytime, or Mr. Sandman. My usual check-in time is late afternoon, and it would seem I'm the only transient in town, but tomorrow morning the parking lot is sure to be lined with vehicles. They offer clean, comfortable space, even that boxcar back in Erie with the spacious lawn and lovely shade trees—ever thankful for the unused pepper spray.

Paid a visit to the Minot Zoo this afternoon, a perfect day to experience the pure joy of lemonade. Spent time with a half-sociable coyote. When I approached her enclosure, she slinked to a tree covered shelter, but my walking away brought her back to the gate, watching me intently until I turned her way—*Here-and-Gone*. We played that game for a while as a Musk Ox looked on from a nearby pen, standing straight and still in the sun, eyes closed, toes together, proud of its shaggy coat and sensible ox shoes.

Tomorrow I head for the Badlands then south to Medora, crossing the border into Montana, and to Miles City by the weekend where I plan to spend a week, including the little town called Hathaway twenty miles beyond, and Rosebud, "Look for three buildings," Sheridan, Wyoming, after that.

Wednesday, June 19th
The Four Eyes Motel, Watford City, North Dakota—$23.54

Decided to wash some clothes, so somewhere between Minot's Ho-Hum Motel and the Badlands west of here, I chose the town of Stanley. The approach to Dakota's west end is a gradual drift into hill country, and June breezes out here do more than rustle your shirt, a chilly reminder that Canada is not so far to the north. AM radio reports include cattle, hog and lamb prices, and discussions of a recently approved insecticide meant to aid farmers in protecting grain crops, late this year because of the rain.

I'd say she's about eighty with a classic granny face. She remarked that I was a long way from home as she emptied a washer, filling two peach baskets with wet clothes, "A good day to use the clothesline." In another time and place I'd call her Jessica Tandy.

Five will get me more this Laundromat is for sale. It's barely maintained and someone who'd like to be rid of it is forced to keep it going. But it washes and dries, and the washers clean themselves where it matters. Reading material consists of the *Minot Daily News*, *Readers Digest*, *The Lutheran* and *Our Daily Bread*. Other patrons have departed, and alone in a western laundry I'm still asking: where is this odyssey headed, and what will come of it? Despair has yet to even pull at my sleeve. Now and then a bit of longing for home, but so far, no urge to turn back, no real anxiety except for my chronic fear of a flat tire in the middle of nowhere. Does 911 ring through Dakota?

Another Granny heard from, this one clad in classic seventies polyester. Pale pink knit slacks with stitched front seams topped off with a jacket striped vertically in shades of magenta, lavender, blue, orange, yellow and, of course, pale pink to match the pants. She wore thin white ankle socks and brown medium heel shoes, and her hair, the color of henna, is kept in place with a thin nylon scarf tied at the chin, "necessary these days with all this blowin'."

She carried her soap and fabric softener in Cheez Whiz jars. As she sorted through the darks and lights, I studied the clothing labels, a practice acquired from my days at Pittsfield Weaving Company— woven labels finished from the looms in various cuts depending on the garment it will be sewn into, millions of them shipped every day to the mills down south: straight cut, cut/fold, mitre/fold, satin, taffeta, shuttle or broadloom, 32mm—the mind-set will never leave. There it was, stitched into Norma's clothing—black on white, taffeta straight cut, the *Copy Cat* label, ordered out of the Garment District on 7th Avenue, NYC, designed and woven in Pittsfield, New Hampshire, shipped to a mill in North Carolina and stitched to this very collar that finds itself in Stanley, North Dakota.

The plate glass windows here are streaked with the prints of children. The heat register, clogged with matted gray dust pillows, pushes upward from the floor at an odd angle, as if from a tiny earthquake. *Out Of Order* signs shout from various dryer doors at alarming intervals. Which one might perform for these quarters?

Norma is a retired teacher. Her husband died back in 1968 at the age of fifty-nine, and her four children brought her through it. At one time they farmed nine hundred acres of wheat and raised cattle as well. She now works four days a week at the local rest home, teaching and entertaining the residents. This weekend she's going to see Billy Graham on a bus tour to Minneapolis.

"Joyce's Café is where you should go for lunch," she said, the diner in the center of town. At noon it was nearly filled with an assortment of ranchers, town fathers and young men sitting wherever there was space. The waitress approached each group, patting one on the shoulder calling out today's special, or "Hey, George, you want the meatloaf today?" They were talking shop, "Too much spring rain…wheat crop's late…replace it with soybeans…something getting caught in the machinery, dying in the fields, smelling up the wind rows."

I was the *alien* taking up the space of an entire booth, which seemed at this moment the size of a small pasture. Where's my gregarious sister when I need her? She'd own the room like Barbara Walters in a matter of minutes. Folks coming in would join the earthlings in various empty slots because the *alien is there* consuming meatloaf the size of four decks of cards, mashed potato, gravy, corn bread with butter and a *jug* of coffee. Perhaps I'll jus' go on out thar' and clean up them stinkin' wind rows! ***Time-Out:*** *Windrow: a row of hay raked up to dry before being baled or stored.*

Can't believe that five hours and 150 miles later I'm munching bread sticks here at the "Four Eyes Motel" in Watford City. I'm preparing to head south through the Badlands, an auto tour through Theodore Roosevelt National Park—***that*** four-eyes. Previews of the Black Hills were spotted in random smidges from the interstate, muted forms materializing in solitary buttes, postcard clouds across the sky.

Road construction was underway just ahead of the Little Missouri River crossing, the bridge over sage green water. Flag persons in these parts are Native American women, smiling with their signs that say SLOW. The lingering memory of Dakota next winter, after the journey has ended, the lingering memory will be of straight roads, endless before me, vista to vista, here a horse, there a herd, the tiny ramshackle church on a gravel road tilted against the sky at the crest of a hill, all to the song of rustling grasses and wind with substance.

According to Norma back at the Laundromat, its owners have tried to sell the place more than once, having owned it more than thirty years—needs work indeed, as well as dryers that produce heat. My clean wet clothing was bounced among three inept machines, so I waited for Norma's departure and used hers to finish the job, except for the still damp jeans that hang from the window of my car, flipping in the wind outside the Four Eyes Motel.

Signed, *Drying in Dakota*

Thursday, June 20
The Bel Vu Motel, Belfield, North Dakota—$28.08

Checked out of the *Four Eyes* this morning and soon found a nice young man at Friendly Al's who smilingly agreed to check the air in my tires, a lingering concern, flat tire phobia—have I mentioned that before? However, I should feel at least somewhat prepared, what with this handy how-to booklet, *Essential Car Care: Do It!* Right off the bat it says: "loosen lug nuts." So I smiled at Friendly Al, praying he would enhance my peace of mind without an attitude like that guy back in Devil's Lake who was not having a good day. Wilfred Hathaway would have checked the tires, and *then* some. He would have explained tire pressure, etc. etc…how to use the gauge, etc… you don't know how to check the tire pressure yourself? Do you even have a pressure gauge? Can't believe at your age you've never blah blah blah…what if you broke down in the middle of nowhere? Oh, that's right! I'm *IN* the middle of nowhere!

Mud Pies

Masterpieces have twice the impact when come upon without warning. It happened back in New Hampshire when I first drove through Dixville Notch. The Balsams is a magnificent north woods hotel and resort, a luminous Italian villa that seems to raise itself from the woods at the bend of the road. Leaving Watford City this morning, I was headed for the north unit of Theodore Roosevelt National Park. My mind drifted from one panorama to the next when they appeared abruptly at all sides, mounds of brown earth, layers of lava rock, gray, red and tan, dressed with grasses and scrub pine. The undulating hot top curved and sliced through ripples of volcanic matter, sculpted in shale and sandstone—Dixville Notch meets mud pies on the moon. This is *Gordon-back-home* country, the science guy who'd have long names for all this geology and, by the way, a shameless punster who might say I was *waxing sedimental.*

Meandering through the mesas, bison dot the slopes like boulders, *raw umber* straight from the tube. A lone bull grazed nearby while another rolled blissfully in a dust puddle beside the road, accustomed to vehicles like moose and deer back home. Nature trails are mowed in yard-wide swaths toward overlooks above the Little Missouri River. Wood roses, yarrow, and prickly pear cacti line the pathways, reminding me at once of Aunt Alice, my lifelong professor of bird-watching and wildflowers who's been known to *borrow* a Lady Slipper or two for her own backyard forest. Had Robert Frost *stopped by those woods* in springtime, there's a whole lot he might have penned on Jack-in-the-Pulpit, Skunk Cabbage, dandelion greens and breaks, or is it fiddleheads? But that's for later discussion, a different culinary issue altogether, right up there with brussels sprouts and tripe. Don't even get her started.

A lot of time is spent searching for words other than breathtaking and beautiful. Adequate language is lacking. Where's *Trina-Back-Home*, crossword and Boggle maven? The butte is beautiful? A couple celebrating their forty-ninth anniversary stood at an overlook snapping pictures of one another, so I offered to document their presence together.

Driving through the park, I noticed a lone bison standing on a ridge halfway up a jagged slope, as if placed on the narrow shelf by a crane for park display. How did he get his bulk up there? When I drove through an hour or two later, he was still lounging in the sun. If this is any indication of raw beauty, as in beautiful, then Butch and Marie-back-home are going to love the Grand Canyon next summer. I often razz Butch about his Homer Simpson attention span. I imagine him standing at an overlook, nodding with approval, "Nice view... let's go, Dear." No, I believe he'll linger a few minutes with his saintly wife. The rosary beads she gave me are worn by Travel Mouse, another good luck companion named Christopher. They sit together in the car: Christopher with White Dog, the one tinged with St. Bernard spit, anointed by Mack-back-home. The crystal from Jan hangs from the rearview mirror, and the tiny Cabbage Patch angel from Pat hovers from a door handle. All of these bless me with good fortune as evidenced by *Friendly Al* back there in Watford City who checked the tires.

Stopped for lunch at The Four Corners Café out on 23 West, a culinary oasis set at the crossroads in a sea of whatever was growing, five or six pickups in a line outside. I was starving. Folks in truck stops have whatever's on the board, just like Joyce's place back there in Stanley. Beef indeed is what's for dinner, and mashed potato with gravy. Wendy's Salad Bar? Not among these amber waves. Soup today was potato dumpling. If "it ain't over 'til the fat lady sings," I'll be gearing up soon for that checkup in November, hoping a couple of months will be long enough for lipid trimming. Tomorrow, Medora at the South Unit of the park, and the border crossing into Montana after that. Approaching apogee so soon? Losing hope for finding insulators, however. Hathaway is practically a ghost town according to Juanita of Rosebud; perhaps a secondhand shop somewhere along the way. Do they call them that anymore?

Friday, June 21
The El Centro Motel, Glendive, Montana—$23.90

I shouldn't be doing this. I've met with disappointment before when a so-called magic photo has come to the fore. The print develops in my head, its image imbedded before film leaves the camera. But I see him so clearly, the magnificent buffalo, the real deal *Itinerary Bison* on the roadside as I descended an overlook, standing in profile, part of the plan. He was yards away, paying me no mind, placed there just for me on Teddy's Magic Ride. *Stop the car. Point and shoot!* Imagination inflates me. I just photographed the cover of next year's "Dakota Travel Guide," and won't they thank me for this totally original idea, a bison on the cover of South Dakota's travel guide. Well, you are welcome, South Dakota!

Poo—It happens. The south unit of the park twists and turns for thirty miles through towering mud cakes and petrified ruins, pillars of silt and stone in ruffled skirts topped with adobe gargoyles. Today's nature trail is steeper, a rougher upward climb, nearly stepped in a buffalo pie. Truly breathtaking! No, really, my breath! But at the end of the climb I found a single bench and sat atop the butte with miles of chaparral to ponder alone—I and a number of Prairie Dogs. Quote of the Day: ***Watch your step*** at the home where the buffalo roam.

> **Peaceful Valley Ranch**
> **Trail Rides—A Wilderness Riding Adventure**
> **Seven Miles North in Theodore**
> **Roosevelt National Park**
>
> "Horseback riding is classified as a rugged adventurous recreational sport activity and you will be riding in a wilderness environment. There are inherent risks in horseback riding. You should become aware of these risks before participation. Know your abilities and limitations. We do not guarantee your safety. Some elements would include, but are not limited to: wildlife, weather, terrain, and horse's natural instincts. Must weigh under 240 pounds…must fit in western saddle with no overlap.

Difficult decision to make under this big sky: to *rough ride* or not to? Perhaps later, down in Kansas or Texas, back in New Hampshire maybe at Castle in the Clouds—memories still fresh of that horse in Aruba, definitely a maverick of "natural instincts."

*****

Ode to My Horse on a Beach in Aruba

The ride began serenely
As we trotted thru the cacti
This ain't so bad after 25 years,
At that point a matter of facti.
In golden light and trade winds calm
Beside the quiet sea,
The ride was downright splendid
Till my horse dropped to his knees.
And after he rolled about in the sand,
Giving his back a scratch,
He stood and nipped the horse in front,
And after that, kicked the one in back,

And whether I asked him to or not,
He danced around every chance he got!
Then down he went to the sand once more
For a wallow in the sunset
And into a dune again I was tossed,
(hard to ignore such an upset)
Get right back on, I said to myself
And show him who's the boss.
And that's when I leaned real close to his ear
And said with damn little remorse,
I ain't gettin' off till this ride is done,
*So **move it**, you fucking horse!*

Montana

Sat, Sun, Mon, Tues, Wed, June 22 to 26
Motel 6, Miles City, Montana—$28.07 per night

Five days will be spent here in Miles City, time to breathe, develop photos, identify certain panoramas for the writing later. The main event this weekend was to be its Annual Balloon Roundup, but Sunday morning was the only flight scheduled and weather would become a problem. When I drove down to the field that morning at five thirty it was New Hampshire cool, and the voice of Alan Jackson blasted across the grounds. Clouds pushed off to the east, and a stubborn wind continued to gust, so after a brief meeting it was announced that liftoff was "at pilot discretion." Five balloons went aloft and disappeared over a distant mesa. Chase vehicles have it easy out here under this big sky. There's the balloon, go get the balloon, quite different from New England's hills and valleys and landing in someone's backyard or a remote pond two towns away. The wind picked up some more, and the loosely packed group of onlookers scattered.

Sat yesterday in the parking lot at the Miles City Livestock Commission, a busy place on this auction Tuesday as trailer after trailer arrived with small committees of stock. Rusty metal gates create temporary corrals for the nervous animals. One trailer deposited a large bull that bellowed his anxiety across the yard, while in the next lot, several white-faced bovines with curly red fur and long white lashes seemed to pay him little mind. Now and then someone would come by on horseback, scanning the small groups, slapping them with an adhesive tag, sending them along—like cattle—into corrals that disappear into a connecting shed where horsemen coax and whistle.

The Range Riders Museum is located just up the road from the stockyards. Homer Holmes might be eighty or more and likes to help out at the museum. He wore dungarees, western boots, a white cotton shirt, suspenders, and a cowboy hat. He stood next to an antique cash register in a large room lined across its upper beams with heads of bison, elk, and deer, and perched above its many display cases, a collection of hawks, falcons and an angry eagle. Saddles lined one wall, and above them hung rows of chaps, ropes, and spurs. Homer spoke with a slow drawl, of when he was young back in '19 working the plains. I photographed him beside the cash register and in front of the museum. He explained the operation of the Livestock Commission and the auction sales that go on there. When I went back later, the trading was done, the grounds quiet, the corrals empty, except for a couple of camera shy horses dancing nervously in a small shed.

An advance pilgrimage to the town of Hathaway was made yesterday. I couldn't wait any longer. It's located twenty miles west of Miles City, a railroad crossing visible from the interstate, along with the roofs of two or three buildings, one of them, the former post office that Juanita McDanold wrote about last fall from the town of Rosebud further west. The other building is the Hathaway Bar where several horse trailers were parked. Do I simply walk into a bar in this former town? *Hi, I just drove here from New Hampshire 'cause I'm a Hathaway and thought it'd be really cool to say I'd been here.* I drove across the tracks following a gravel road that led to a farm beyond. A small herd of Black Angus watched NH 12741 pass by. No people, but I picked up a few Hathaway rocks for me and the sibs.

But Homer Holmes knows Hathaway. "Jim Patrick owns that bar in Hathaway, so you jus' go on down thar tomorrow and stop in. Tell him Homer sent you. Women sit at the bars out here all the time…me and the wife go to Hathaway just for the dance floor on *Saturdee* night…I play the fiddle, you know." Having seen a room filled with insulators at the Range Riders Museum, and now with a *Homer-Sent-Me Pass* to downtown Hathaway, is finding a spare insulator possible? It's one notch above a ghost town, rundown enough, maybe there'd be one or two lying around. That would take this journey beyond dreams. Again, the itinerary says it, so it must be so "… south into Hathaway, seeking one more insulator for Dad."

"Go right straight to Hathaway," Homer echoed, "and have a talk with Jim Patrick." I did one last drive through Miles City, past the Bison Bar and the Montana Bar. Men in cowboy hats cross the street before me or nod from a pickup truck. Doesn't matter who you are out here, you're waved at. Casinos and bars blink, and the water tower with a bucking bronco logo reaches above the cottonwood grove in the park where children splash water crystals to the sky.

Passed the *600 Cafe* where I experienced chicken fried steak the day before. Can't help recalling the young boy seated near the cash register as I was leaving. His greeting lingers vividly in my mind, replaying like film, "How's your day today, ma'am?" he said, with a polite nod and an earnest smile, hat resting on his knee, looking straight into my eyes through at least four decades, a twelve-year-old to pay attention to—can't come up with a comparable adult-child back home. "How's your day, ma'am?" Driving past the Livestock Commission and the Range Riders Museum, I nodded to Mr. Holmes. When I gave him a small bottle of NH Maple Syrup, he in turn promised to mail me one of his handmade *H Brand* key rings.

Time-Out— *"Chicken Fried Steak is an item not likely to make it onto many white tablecloth menus, and it's never made it onto fast food menus either. But in the cafeterias and lunch counters of Alabama and Arkansas, the Tex-Mex eateries in Houston,* *and the bars and grills across the plains, you still find this crunchy, delightful dish. They make it the right way—cheap, tenderized beef, a dredging that adheres and turns golden brown and juicy, usually served with a hot, peppery milk gravy on top and some freshly whipped potatoes and butter on the side, along with a biscuit or two, some overcooked string beans, and a pitcher of iced tea."*

—Restaurant Take-Out Menu

- 1 egg
- 2 cups milk
- 1 tsp Tabasco brand pepper sauce
- 1 cup flour
- Salt & pepper
- 4 slices round steak

Beat together the egg, milk and *Tabasco*. Season the flour to taste with salt and pepper (the mixture should be peppery). Pound steak slices until thin and tender, then dip in egg mixture. Dredge in flour mixture and fry in hot shortening until crisp in a black iron skillet. Drain on brown paper bags.

*****

A few vehicles sped past as I dawdled along I-94 in the direction of Hathaway, Montana, setting the scene: So a single woman from back east walks into a bar. Every stool is taken by the cast of *Gunsmoke.* The door swings open and they all turn her way, as in Dodge City: *Hi, she mutters…uh, Homer Holmes sent me. I'm looking for Mr. Patrick.* The parking lot is empty today, but "Hathaway Bar" is lit in neon. No cars, no horse trailers. It's exactly high noon. Here's the doorknob. *Turn the damn knob, Gloria Jean—Homer said!*

Homer had sketched the mental image, and I stepped in. A bar extended to the far end of the room with ten or twelve empty stools. There was an antique cash register shining chrome and brass, and lines of bottles and decanters along the wall, a mirror behind them and a Coke machine wedged nearby. A small bulletin board held business cards, fifty or so tacked to a patch of wall next to the door, not one sign saying *Men Only.*

James C. Patrick was seated behind the bar. He wore a plaid shirt, turquoise and white, with dark blue suspenders. His silver hair was combed straight back, and he sat calmly in the light of the open door, nodding politely as I entered. His calmness, his china blue eyes, and my quick recollection of Hannibal Lecter caused a momentary twinge.

But no, my new best friend nodded and grinned as I rambled on about *Homer-back-there,* that I was a Rhode Island Hathaway. He spoke hesitatingly at first but grew more animated as he described the town "when it used to be a town" with its own grain elevator and train depot. Said he came to the area from a small town in Oklahoma back in the twenties when he was five years old. His wife died three years ago, but together they ran the post office and general store. His face brightened as he recalled their partnership. A room adjacent to the bar had four or five more bar stools, a dart board, a pool table, jukebox, and a small dance floor, probably where Homer plays the fiddle. Mr. Patrick has been "at this for fifty years now," and he's tired. The place is for sale, and until it goes, he lives alone in the former general store and post office next door.

The town was named for George Hathaway, a Civil War veteran who came to the area and made it thrive. On the wall hung a calendar with pictures of Stratford-upon-Avon, home of Anne (Hathaway) Shakespeare and her husband, a writer.

I spoke of my father's travels and his quest for insulators. We talked for an hour or more, and when I asked to take his picture, he dismissed it with a short wave, his not being very photogenic, but whipped out a comb, running it quickly through his white hair, suggesting the cash register might be a good spot. He stood beside a brass plaque: Hathaway Bar.

Time-Out—George W. Hathaway was a first sergeant in Company K. He served through the Civil War and was mustered out in 1865. The present day-Hathaway Bar is Hathaway's claim to fame. Jane Canary, otherwise known as Calamity Jane, stayed there at one time.

All the while, the question pulled at my shirt. *Ask him. Ask him. It's on the itinerary, line 17: "one more insulator for Dad…" to place at his grave, ask him. The Master Weaver said!* When I mentioned insulators, the existence of one here in Hathaway, he shook his head, saying that over the years he'd seen them, "when the railroad was still going, kids used to play with 'em, but the Depot's gone now, not much left." More conversation about life in Montana as I followed him through his living quarters next door to retrieve an envelope he wanted me to see. The space was dingy, cluttered with piles of clothes, the kitchen sink filled with a few pots and dirty plates, definitely missing his wife. The hallway led to a darkened room with dusty wooden chairs and a desk. The envelope was filled with old photos: the Hathaway grain elevator, farms, trains chugging through the depot billowing white smoke, horsemen, rodeo riders and livestock, and his treasure, a faded eight-by-ten tea-stained print of Charlie Russell seated on a wagon, two bison in harness—the other half of the Remington legend, dueling painters. He rose and stacked the photos, putting them back in the tattered envelope.

My mind wanted to linger there a while with Charlie Russell. *So you were a human once, sitting on a wagon seat, bison in rein. What else went on that day? Where were you headed? Did you mentally plan a canvas? Who took the picture? What kind of camera? Later, man down in the Cowboy Hall of Fame.*

We were running out of conversation, and my awkward self felt the need to move on. When I rose to leave, stating the obligatory, "I want to thank you, Mr. Patrick, for spending this time," "Wait a second," he spoke quietly, "wait here just a minute while I have a look." He went outside while I waited in the bar, alone on a bar stool, *on hold* in Hathaway, Montana. I knew what he was looking for. It's on the itinerary, the moose at dusk, the magic insulator, and *Graceland* farther along. All is quiet on this cosmic western front, here in a bar far from home waiting for an object I decided three years earlier was waiting somewhere in Hathaway just for me, a strangely quiet few minutes in a remote ghost town. So it hardly seemed surreal that the jukebox in the *ballroom* next door would suddenly play. Waiting, watching cattle graze in a pasture beyond, a distant silent film with crows on the fence mouthing noiseless caws—quiet, quiet, then a clicking sound from the next room, a silent DJ, cue *The Eagles: "Welcome to the Hotel California."*

What prompted the eccentric jukebox into song, barely causing a jar to my frame of mind, as if such an event were commonplace? It's still a startling event in retrospect. Through the grimy window just above the dance floor in the other room, I could see Mr. Patrick rummaging through some things on the ground, as now and then his silver hair and plaid collar would appear, then lower out of sight, searching hurriedly, bending, looking, and when the brown door finally opened, he leaned forward to place three grimy insulators at my feet. Not one, but three "grails"—one clear glass, one aquamarine, and one of solid brown. The *wayward* Eagles went off script in the next room…

> There he stood in the doorway;
> When I heard the Depot bell
> And I was thinking to myself,
> "This could be Heaven, *or not, I couldn't tell*"
> There were voices down the corridor,
> And I heard *Rod Serling* say…

Welcome to this, the *Hotel Hathaway*
Such a lovely place…*a magical space…*

The moving finger wrote this mind-blowing scenario three years ago, another hand, I've believed all along. Destiny is a word not truly understood by me, until now, the extraordinary summer of '96. What next, perhaps an Elvis sighting? Who will stand in line with me at Graceland on that Friday in August? Why should any of this cause hesitation, even that dawn stroll across Brooklyn's span. Have I mentioned the bridge before?

*****

"Dream as if you'll live forever. Live as if you'll die today."—*James Dean*

On this day in June, the images of Juanita McDanold and James Dean the myth were sealed forever in my memory. This first came about last year through my letter of inquiry about the town and its services, sent to the attention of *Postmaster, Hathaway, MT*. She reported the alarming news, handwritten on yellow-lined paper:

> *"I am sorry to inform you the Hathaway Post Office is closed. I am the Postmaster at Rosebud about ten miles away. There is no place to stay overnight in either Hathaway or Rosebud. There is a bar in Hathaway, a rural community, mostly farming and cattle. I wish you a safe and splendid journey. Please do stop in at Rosebud to chat if you can. We are a small town also. We have a school, Bar-Café and Post Office. Best Regards, Juanita McDanold."*

Since then, I had imagined the little town of Rosebud and Postmaster Juanita McDanold, her image building in my mind: six-tyish, short, rotund, hair pulled back in a bun, welcoming me to Montana, apologizing for the sorry condition of Hathaway. From the interstate, the town appeared larger than I had imagined. The small post office is on the main street and had been painted recently. "Are you Juanita?" I asked. The blonde woman answered tentatively. *How should I know this person,* she's thinking. I recalled our exchange of letters last year, prompting a smile.

Hindsight: Stereotyping can often be right on! *Not!*

In another time and place she might be Sandra Dee, and James Dean was looking very James Dean on a poster promoting the new stamp in his memory, rebellious, brooding across time, forever young in the postal window beside her. As I snapped a photo  through the oak frame, she was typecast again: Juanita McDanold, prom queen, most likely to date James Dean; Postmaster, Rosebud, Montana, population 175.

We discussed the giant cottonwood tree next to the building, seen as a sapling in a 1916 photograph on the wall. It was struck by lightning in a recent storm, the slash down its trunk rerouted slightly by the presence of a railroad spike embedded in the trunk; shreds of bark scattered the ground.

The town of Forsyth twenty miles west was named for Civil War General James W. Forsyth. It has a longer main street than Rosebud and boasts a variety of storefronts, so I shopped for a picnic lunch at the grocery store and headed for a park at the Yellowstone River. Seated on a rock beneath a cottonwood tree, the steady rush of its pale green water triggered a soothing meditation where Joey's Montana stone caught my attention. Tomorrow, the Little Bighorn.

Thursday, June 27
The Camp Custer Motel, Hardin, Montana—$25.00 (cash only)

My furthest point west is reached here in the town of Hardin, on the road to Custer Battlefield, but my spirit took a greater leap on this day, a process of overcoming minor hesitations—*Madame Cowardice* pushes herself across another border.

I'm trackside again in a most affordable room, twenty-five dollars a night, cash only, and it's hard to settle down when a freight train roars past every thirty minutes. Its haunting whistle is a summons, and I stand at the door for each train, counting cars, while my twelve-year-old soul returns to Slocum, Rhode Island's crossing, again, where I and my sister wave to the engineer, waiting for the red caboose. Train whistles and foghorns, if I haven't said this before, are downright *narcotical*; and, one more time, the same goes for the aroma of cow barns and low tide across Narragansett Bay. Tried to call my sister; however, Judy was not her chatty phone self on this magical evening. While it was still daylight in Hardin, I failed to remember that 8:30 p.m. in Hardin, Montana, is ten thirty in Newport, Rhode Island, and her labored efforts at conversation gave me a clue. Later, Jude.

Don't look now, but two out of three occupants residing here at Camp Custer hail from New England: NH 12741 and—be sure to pronounce this with proper New England annoyance—*a Massachusetts driver!* I never did meet 959-YKM as all three occupants turned in early.

CHAPTER 23

Wyoming

Friday, Saturday and Sunday, June 28, 29, 30
The Triangle Motel, Sheridan, Wyoming—$21.60 per night

Took a quick drive around the Custer Battlefield this morning, its acres of white stones spread like the markers at Normandy. Caught a lecture on the ammunition used to that grisly end, not that long ago really, the last surviving warriors died in the fifties. A peaceful hill of grasses and yellow clover meet darkening clouds across the expanse to the Little Bighorn River, dotted randomly with white stones, one was marked "Goes Ahead, Custer Scout, May 31, 1919."

The Triangle Motel off the main drag here in Sheridan is a deal, come upon with the usual shop-by-bag phone. This one has the look of a neglected villa. Overgrown flowerbeds skirt the drive and adjacent courtyard with hollyhocks, sunflowers, and leggy bachelor's buttons. Cedar trees with gnarled trunks stand beside each brightly colored door matched with orange fiberglass chairs, circa 1955. I was greeted by an elderly Native American. His long gray hair was tied back, and he wore painter's pants with a ragged T-shirt. I was ushered to my prospective room to decide "if it was suitable." He didn't understand: rustic, overgrown, cheap, this is the Ritz! The resident bulldog completed the greeting, tomorrow's dream photo: Bulldog with Native American in vintage fiberglass chair.

Its owner told me she's been in operation since the sixties and has met many travelers looking for a three or four-day home, some of them taking part in the reenactment at Little Bighorn. Her softly permed silver hair was tied back from her face with a pink scarf, and she had an animated way of rambling from one story to another as she gathered an assortment of faded towels, my three-day allotment. A take-charge, "make the best with what you've got" lady, she was good theater, and in another time and place I'd call her one of the *Golden Girls,* Blanche, I think.

The truth is, I'm a *female* today, looking for reasons to be sad. Poor me, "Alone, alone, all, all alone..." Never thought I'd say this, but Peter Joseph, son of mine, make that face, the one that "enhanced" so many of our family pictures. A foghorn or the howl of a freight train would really drive this home.

> *Note to Self: In Pembroke, NH, your ass on the couch, you'd still be alone. Back in New Hampshire, the Bighorn Mountains aren't in your backyard.*
>
> *PS: "We live as we dream—alone."*
>
> —*Joseph Conrad (again)*

*****

The Pearl Harbor Connection, Saturday, June 29

The morning couldn't have been more inspiring for its energy and light, and I left the door open so as not to miss anything. The punched-faced dog appeared at the threshold and sat on the stoop demonstrating his sinus malady, breathing in and out with loud snores. Wearing a trim carpet of tan, his large eyes bulged from a graying black mask, and when I spoke to him he smiled broadly with each inward breath as his tongue curled in a full wide roll. Standing here snoring was one half of the dream photo as *Walks-With-Shovel* soon crossed the courtyard to tend the flower beds. There's that destiny thing again, always at my shirt. *Ask him, get the camera!*

"Walks-With-Shovel" is not of the Lakota tribe. Born in Hawaii in 1913, he was a civilian worker with the Navy when Pearl Harbor was bombed. I told him I was born that day, but it didn't catch his attention—he was telling the story.

Joseph Cumalaa was preparing for a drive into town that morning in 1941 to begin work when he received the news. "We were bombed," they told him. He shrugged, "We're bombed all the time—drills!" He was there, at Pearl, on December 7 when America's history shuddered across the sea, and when my hand swung toward the car pointing to my date of birth on its plate, he jumped slightly, reading it aloud, "The same year!" This would explain the instantaneous addition of another branch to the Hathaway family tree, begat through a magical Pearl Harbor moment in North Central Wyoming.

J. K. Bird, he calls himself (because no one pronounces *koom-a-LA-ah* correctly), left Hawaii in 1973. He had opened an unidentified canister of Agent Orange, an action that lead to months of recovery and chronic ill health. And the bulldog is not a bulldog, but an aging pug who sat in on a couple of photos, panting with sad smiles. The dog is adjusting to life without his longtime companion, a *pug-ette*, put down three months before. This knowledge magnified even more the sadness of his lonesome face.

Sits-with-Car (Uncle Joe) was photographed in a fiberglass chair the color of tangerine beside NH 12741, Live Free or Die. I love this country!

Saturday errands today: laundry, quick lube, film stop. Exiting Wal-Mart will never be the same. Pushing from its doors in Sheridan, Wyoming reveals a panorama of the snowcapped Bighorn Mountains, tomorrow's day trip.

Signed, *Dame of Infamy*

Monday, July 1, the Bighorns

Cattle herds along the interstate huddle for shade in small groups beside the occasional billboard. Had to pass up what could have been a dandy photo out on the highway, virtual lunches, grazing beneath a Burger King sign along the eastbound lanes.

Drove from Dayton, Wyoming, elevation 3,900 feet at the base of the Bighorns, toward Lovell on the west side of the range, a real mix at elevation 9,400 feet, wild flowers and jagged ridges of 500-million-year-old rock formations, unsettling displays of prior *falling rocks* that lay perilously close to the inside lane. At the top, miles of pastureland and interesting signs: Open Range–Loose Stock.

Caution, Bighorn traffic. Cattle cross the road at the top of this world, another middle of nowhere. The young ones lagging behind seemed to dawdle purposely, testing patience, a juvenile trait I recall vividly because in another time and place those calves would be Trina's kid, Gabe, and my son Pete. Random carpets of snow clung to the upper slopes in large slabs like sourdough starters for next season, a reminder of the icebergs back in Michigan. In the distance a small herd raced across a field to the tree line, too far off to identify. The middle of nowhere has been reached. Or was it the top of the stairs at Sullys Hill in Dakota? Or Hathaway, Montana, less three insulators, two rusty railroad spikes and five rocks?

Said good-bye to Helen Olsen at the Triangle Motel this morning. Uncle Joe was not around, but we said our good-byes last evening after he talked some more about Pearl: "Won't forget...not ever forget it! Still like yesterday. I knew many of them down there on the Arizona. And you know, Mr. Elvis Presley, he pay for that memorial." Across the highway, a flock of white birds flew upward into the blinding sunlight. He had never seen them before, shading his eyes, wondering what they were, in awe of the sight. I recalled South Florida's dining egrets.

*****

Gillette, Wyoming, July 1

I'm Bart Simpson today writing on the board: *I do not want to smoke I do not want to smoke I do not want to smoke I do not want to smoke I do not want to smoke*

Time-out! Why, having quit twelve years ago, do I want a cigarette?

a) isolation
b) free as a bird in another cage
c) fear of the unknown, what lies ahead
d) a week off hormones
e) two months to go, can I go the distance?
f) will I find Brooklyn's bridge?
g) what I just said.

Back in Montana I stopped along the interstate to photograph a sunflower growing from the baked pavement. Magenta has been on my mind—*frail woman, hear her roar,* afraid of what's ahead, almost a PhD but not, worried about where to go—back to the family in the Seattle area or back to San Diego. This thriving sunflower will make a perfect postcard for Magenta of Minneapolis, a token nudge of encouragement—talk about the *pot calling the kettle.*

Getting the shot became more of an event than planned when I was approached by the Montana State Police. There's that *Manda Syndrome* again. Manda was our St. Bernard, our *first child* whose largeness was often blamed for objects ending up on the floor in loud crashes. So much so that loud noises of any kind, even in space not occupied by the cow-in-the-house, triggered a swift departure, her massive head hanging low, ears drooping, eyes painfully red and ashamed, trotting toenails punctuating her swift exit to anywhere else: *If it crashed and broke, I must have done it.*

Must have been speeding, I thought. I pulled over, and in the time it took for him to exit his vehicle and walk to my car, my inner sixth grader imagined a consequence: *Can I pay this fine with a credit card? What are the rates out here? Will I have to go to court? Do I know how fast I was going? Well no. There's nothing here but highway and that big deal Big Sky.* I rolled the window down, a humble, obliging *eldress.* He leaned forward to ask if everything was OK. As it turned out, he'd spotted my car from across the highway and crossed the median to check on the circumstances of NH 12741. How to answer this one. *I was photographing that sunflower back there growing out of the SEEment—that's how they say it out here.*

"I'm fine…everything's OK, thank you, just taking a picture." He drove away. Sigh of relief, deep breath. Jim's out there in the cosmos shaking his head again. *That heavy foot of yours, I don't know how you get away with it…If I did that…blah…blah…*

Magenta! Just look at this piece of harsh, baked pavement with nothing to offer but a glorious sunflower! You'll get beyond this rough patch and blossom. The likes of you could never go to seed!

Signed, Whistling-in-the-Dark,
I do not want to smoke.

South Dakota

Wednesday, July 3, Rapid City, South Dakota
Avanti Motel, $37.75

This has been coming for nearly a week now, best I just come out with it. *Agony of Defeat,* I thought at first when the taunts began. No, just a lapse, a setback; I should have better prepared. It's a good thing I read *Travels with Charley* twice: once in my twenties: *What a cool thing to do!* And again last year: *God, I hope I won't die.*

Mr. Steinbach warned me about it more than once, and here it is, head on: ***That*** "desolate loneliness." It seems to have paralyzed me for a bit, a temporary emotional pothole. It happens to everybody. Take the hormones. Move on!

Time-Out—Pierre, the capital of South Dakota, is not pronounced *pee-AIR*. It's *PEER!* I heard it on the radio. Hope you folks in Mackinac City are reading this.

Three plus years of planning failed to cover all bases for this journey, except maybe the title: "Solitude, Hot Flashes, Other Exhilarations," an insightful description, if I do say so. But the rest of it is to this odyssey what a playbill is to theater, a sweeping sketch, and most days, I'm driving outside the lines. If it's on the itinerary, it took place, and then some, beginning with that moose showing up precisely at dusk, wading in the bog, turning toward my camera as planned.

I-Bison, the Sequel appeared at the top of a mesa, perfect casting, as Buffalo Bull stepped forward at the sound of my approach, this time as I rounded a downward curve. He stood before me in profile, just the two of us, the Badlands his backdrop, billowing white clouds and blue sky. In retrospect, it did seem a bit tidy, his brown coat appeared groomed, no shaggy pelts hanging down, curls fluffed up around his perfectly arched horns shining in the sun. *Places, every-one...but again, do watch your step.*

Poor planning back in Belle Fourche added to this feeling of missing the mark. Reservations should definitely have been made for this Fourth of July in a rodeo town during rodeo week. I was lucky to have had one night there at the Ace Motel ($35.64), a venue most remembered now for last evening's distant thunderstorm, pushing across the plain like a portable room, lightning exploding within, a traveling one-night stand of a show.

Hung out for a while at the roundup this morning. The three-day rodeo starts tomorrow, and the cast was gathering at the grounds—horses, very large bulls and steers, all milling about various corrals as horsepersons separated the herds, driving them into fencing beyond, waiting for curtain. Who in the entertainment business might translate their backstage animal chat? Jeff Foxworthy out in these parts most likely, and it would have to include discussions of cow curls and eyelashes. I believe that indeed bulls *will* make passes at cows with such lashes. Get real, ladies. The lashes don't matter. And those horses, locks fluttering seductively in the breeze, white ones, black ones, paints, and one that suggested a hybrid: equine/canine, a leggy Dalmatian with a long face, full white coat and spots scattered from head to toe. Am I the only one to see it? This horse screams for a chance to lead the Rodeo Parade. I see a red saddle blanket, maybe some faux black boots, an antique fire wagon in tow, the *reining* Rodeo Queen waving from the wagon seat, a real Dalmatian at her side.

Time-Out—Here's how it works: An ox is a mature castrated male belonging to the domestic cattle family, trained to work, and at the end of its life used for meat. A steer is also a castrated male, but younger, not strong enough for hard work; in the United States a steer is not considered an ox until it is four years old.

If Miles City, Montana, and Sheridan, Wyoming, could be likened to Concord, NH, then Rapid City is Providence, a chore to get through riding such a mood. A string of motels with titles in *frugalese* line the interstate across seven exits to this "Gateway to the Black Hills," Econo-this and Budget-that, so I drove to the center of town and phoned for a home. The Avanti Motel is not like the plains rooms back in Montana, but for the extra ten dollars, I'm losing myself with CNN, a microwave and fridge, two double beds, a typing table, and soothing cool air. On the other side of this door stalks the very heat wave that grips the west, while New England has dipped to the frigid seventies.

So, Wilfred, where do I go from here? Where do I take in the fireworks on this Independence Day? Rushmore, perhaps? No cheap motels for the next week, me thinks—tourist havens everywhere. A solitary baking cow stood head on to a billboard along the interstate, as if reading the small print: "rates may vary according to season."

Signed, *Looks-for-Spirit*

Ultimately, I was better placed on this Independence Day than expected. The Belle Fourche rodeo crowd filled that town, so I continued south through Keystone, a gaudy welcoming strip to Mount Rushmore. My soundtrack set the mood as the road curved upward and a jazz version of the *Star-Spangled B* played them into view, granite against Columbia blue, not as wide open a drive-by as expected, though; entering a parking lot must first occur.

The spacious pavilion spreads like an altar before their stone faces, and on this national holiday a troupe of patriots march to fife and drum: *Yankee Doodle, The Battle Hymn,* and *America,* of course. Sunlight illuminates their bright red coats and tri-corner hats with white feather plumes as the small parade passes by. The music cast a spell on this American occasion. Children watched quietly while old veterans stood hand against the heart, the stars and stripes our common thread—parades down Main Street, hostages coming home, John-John's salute, an aching throat.

Crazy Horse Mountain, seen from the visitor's center.

Sculptor Korczak Ziolkowski was born in Boston of Polish descent. Orphaned at age one, he grew up in foster homes. He was self-taught and never took a formal lesson in art, sculpture, architecture, or engineering. When he started work on the mountain in 1949, he was almost forty with little left to his name. He knew at the outset that Crazy Horse was much larger than any one person's lifetime, so he and his wife prepared three books of detailed plans to be used with his scale models to continue the project. "By the time I'm an old lady, the mountain ought to look pretty good," said Monique Ziolkowski, thirty-four, who along with six of her brothers and sisters have stayed to help realize their father's quest. No one involved in the project will hazard a guess as to when the project will reach completion, except to predict the final touches should be made sometime in the 21st century.

The goal is to transform the entire mountain into a sculpture nine stories high, measured from the horse's hoof at the base to a forty-four-foot feather protruding upward from Crazy Horse's headdress. The design is more extensive than Mount Rushmore as the statue will stand eight feet higher than the Washington Monument, and the four presidents' heads together are the size of the great warrior's head, as yet without the flowing hair and single feather (his face alone is eighty-seven feet high and fifty-eight feet wide).

As I remember it, Johnny Hart did a *B.C.* comic strip on sculpting: One cave dweller: "That's a great likeness of Peter. How did you do that?" Sculptor: "Simple, I chipped everything away that doesn't look like Peter." Postcard to Joey: Can't wait to show you the South Dakota rock, blasted clear off the Black Hills.

Thursday, July 4, Custer, South Dakota
Valley Motel, $42.00

Today's room search took a bit more effort in this tourist town on the Fourth of July—finally settled in at the Valley Motel. Guests gathered on the front lawn after dark to watch fireworks explode from the top of a small mountain the shape of a plump traffic cone. Children made new friends, playing tag with loud shrieks in summer's dark while silhouettes sat at picnic tables sipping lemonade, murmuring oooh's with each display—some things are universal.

Wrote a letter to Pete this morning from a laundry in downtown Custer, much fancier than the one back there in Stanley where I and Norma gambled on the strip of heat-challenged appliances.

This one is a video store/laundry combo with hanging plants, tables and chairs, free coffee, and a television playing music videos, at this moment, Jeff Foxworthy's "Party All Night."

Custer State Park is home to one of the largest public-owned herds of bison in the world; more than a thousand of them roam freely throughout the park. I and several other vehicles were driving a slow crawl along the road that meanders through the park when a calf stepped forward from the field, stopping just feet away to study my car. Eye contact was achieved. What's this juvenile processing? Curiosity, boredom, maybe a practice charge at my car? He stood still, fixated, as I reached for the small camera on the seat beside me, a popular *Instamatic* model with the so-called *panorama* format, unused by me until now. In a concentrated effort to move as little as possible, praying he wouldn't run off, I turned slowly to Junior Bison and snapped. He remained in place, while the adult population grazing the prairie beyond far exceeded itinerary dreams. Not the best exposure as it turns out, the only image to survive the roll, so some advance rehearsal in camera setting might have helped, but the photo is a favorite still, mostly for my repeated attempts at reading the animal's thoughts.

Friday, July 5, Martin, South Dakota
The Kings Motel, $37.64

Ran out of accommodating towns south of the Black Hills yesterday and detoured out to Martin, about forty-five minutes east.

The tiny town of Wounded Knee lies a half mile to the west of its burial ground, a bleak "national monument," no parking lots, visitor centers, or gift shops. It sits on a tawny hill seven miles down the road from a blue highway, miles from the interstate. As if to honor my visit, the slope was capped with a dome of rolling gray clouds as I followed a well-worn footpath up to the gate. A light breeze rustled an assortment of cloth tributes, long strips tied to a chain-link fence that separates the mass grave from all the others, a sad, mesmerizing shrine to the 1890 massacre—Lakota's last stand. An apple and an orange lay on the ground near the archway while toasted windswept grasses have overgrown many of the sites. An array of plastic flowers accent the hill, and weather-beaten wood crosses lean toward mounds of hardened clay, adorned with small white stones in curious rows. Toys are placed for the dead children. The more recent graves and contemporary granite markers are scattered among the long gone. A Budweiser bottle leaned against the stone of Marine S Sgt. Vincent Fast Horse, 1975, Vietnam, age twenty-seven.

I sat on a flat rock at the crest of the hill, wrapped in a splendid peace, spiritually adrift in a far-off place, miles from the world beyond. Cattle graze in a neighboring pasture, an entrancing meditation, while a pickup truck passes along the dirt road below, tires crunching the gravel in crisp echoes. From all sides the expanse sings with restless weather, a rickety windmill chattering nearby as I and many grasshoppers share a wondrous moment. The fretful sky seemed to suggest it, so I borrowed a small stone from this sanctuary, to be placed with reverence in the weeks to come next to Hathaway's insulator on my desk back home.

> *"I am tired of talk that comes to nothing. It makes my heart sick when I remember all the good words and broken promises…You might well expect the rivers to run backward as that any man who was born a free man should be contented when penned up and denied liberty to go where he pleases…I have asked some of the great white chiefs where they get their authority to say to the Indian that he shall stay in one place, while he sees white men going where they please. They cannot tell me."*
>
> *—Chief Joseph "Bury My Heart at Wounded Knee," Dee Brown, 1970*

CHAPTER 25

Nebraska

I left Dakota from the Pine Ridge Indian Reservation, crossing the border at Whiteclay, Nebraska, and couldn't resist a brief stop to commune with three horses at the fence. A gray stood as close as barbed wire would allow, enjoying a jaw rub, while the other two, one black and one paint, ambled to and fro with passing interest. The gray nudged my arm if attention slacked off. Took a picture for my sister, the velvet of a horse's nose—just one ♪ of a few ♪ of our favorite things.

Hindsight: The border town of Whiteclay, known to the US Census Bureau as Pine Ridge, has always been tied to the Pine Ridge Indian Reservation located two miles north across the border in South Dakota where alcohol consumption and possession is prohibited.

Saturday/Sunday, July 6 and 7, Chadron, Nebraska
The Roundup Motel, $54.50

The town of Chadron (SHADrun) is located in the panhandle in the northwest corner of the state, and its visitor information director loves his job. Bill is the first human I've met who can discuss *Lonesome Dove* chapter by chapter, and the movie scene by scene. His favorite character is Woodrow Call (Tommy Lee Jones), while I remain spiritually bonded to July Johnson, Chris Cooper in the miniseries, and we agreed that Angelica Huston's ranch in Ogallala would be haven to anyone's spirit. Aside from reading the book, I bought a copy of the six-hour miniseries, and after that, the soundtrack as well as "The Making of Lonesome Dove." Obsessing must be done right.

Bill was most helpful with his suggested maps and five or six brochures. This weekend the Chautauqua Literary Society holds its annual event, an outdoor entertainment under the tent, a reenactment and dramatization of Writers of the Gilded Age. Tomorrow evening's program features Jack London whom I plan to see.

> "....each day mankind and the claims of mankind slipped farther from him. Deep in the forest a call was sounding, and as often as he heard this call, mysteriously thrilling and luring, he felt compelled to turn his back upon the fire and the beaten earth around it, and to plunge into the forest, and on and on, he knew not where or why; nor did he wonder where or why..."
>
> —Jack London

Monday, July 8, Alliance, Nebraska
The Rainbow Motel, $27.00

Six weeks out, and motel rooms and towns are strung together, an energy drought pulling me down. Nutrition, I think—the lack of it—is draining momentum, that or the heat, compounding immobility. Orange juice and bananas are a good start, but avoiding salt and fat is nearly impossible out here. I need to exercise, clear the head. Next week, the halfway mark, heading into Dixie's summer oven. Why did it never enter my mind to map this journey in reverse where at this point, the road home would be across northern borders? It was never a consideration, and for that lapse, I shall always wonder about Lake Superior in July.

Left Chadron this morning after a carwash and map study, headed south through Alliance with its unusual roadside attraction known as *Carhenge*, a collection of junk cars painted gray, planted vertically in the ground at the edge of a corn field. Various groupings are arranged to resemble its ancient stone counterpart in the English countryside. One set of four is titled *The Ford Seasons.*

For fifty miles, cyclers had been seen along the highway through acres of wheat and corn, two and three at a time at first, now and then one resting at the roadside, a mile later three or four more. At *Carhenge* I asked an elder where they were headed. "We left from Seattle," he said, "hope to land in Delaware by August 1, average seventy to a hundred miles a day."

Alliance is located at the west end of Nebraska's Sand Hills, a main room for the Burlington Northern Railroad. As many as a hundred trains pass through town in a twenty-four-hour period, coal cars out of Wyoming headed east to the power plants in Illinois, Missouri and Arkansas, eleven thousand tons in trains over a mile long; grain as well, more than any other railroad.

It's beginning to happen: the name of this motel nearly escaped me. Am I still at the *Roundup* in Chadron or *King's* back there in Martin? That was South Dakota, right? This is the Rainbow Motel in the center of town, no credit cards, tub only, first one with no shower. Air conditioner quiet though, and the best writing desk so far, but no convenient outlet for the word processor; phone, but no direct dial from the room; cable and remote, no channel listing. The Roundup had the History Channel, but no remote. Bedside digital clock handy, but smokers have definitely slept here. Not that I'm above the addictive aroma. As Bonnie back home once said, "For the occasional craving of it, sometimes it smells like apple pie." The addiction of the mind never leaves.

July 9, 10, 11, Ogallala, Nebraska
The Sunset Motel, $73.90

The Sunset Motor Inn was chosen from a short list of *financially feasibles*, no phone the only drawback. A collection of grain elevators loom large, gleaming silver in the sun, and railroad tracks across the road carry the steady rhythm of clacking wheels and whistles that echo for miles.

Chimney Rock is just west of here, "the most famous landmark on the Oregon, California and Mormon Trails." Seeing it today caused me to remember the map on my wall back home with its paste-up of this prairie landmark, it and Miles City being the far-flung high points of my journey to outer space. Cloudy and rainy today, not good for camera work.

On the way to Ogallala, several towns invited me off the highway. Bridgeport's Main Street is lined with a mix of old and new shopping stops, and I met an eldress of the ranching community at the grocery store who paused for a chat. She and her husband farmed for years "with great bounty, never had the trouble that's around these days. Today it's hail. We never lost crops to any hail."

Here was my opportunity to ask what folks out here do with all those kidneys and beef tongue wrapped in cellophane for display in the meat case along with steak and hamburger. Everything we've always wanted to know, but were afraid to ask, about disgusting organ meats was revealed here in the Cornhusker State. "It's a lot like the gizzards, you know, sort of rubbery, you can boil it and make gravy and so forth. It's not for everybody. Myself, I don't like them stomach linings, never would give a go to tripe," she said.

Hindsight: No hail? That had to have been geographic good fortune in the hit and miss of prairie gales.

Nebraska Time-Out: Fresh Tongue, Boiled

Use beef, calf, lamb, or pork tongues, but the best known, beef tongue, may be purchased fresh, smoked, or boiled. The small tongues make delicious dishes that should not be neglected.

Place in kettle: One fresh beef tongue
Peel and add:

- 2 medium onions
- 1 large carrot
- 3 or more ribs of celery with leaves

Wash and add:

- 6 sprigs of parsley

Barely cover these ingredients with boiling water, and add:

- 8 peppercorns
- 1 teaspoon salt

Simmer the tongue until tender, about 3 hours. Drain, reserving the liquor. Skin the tongue. Remove the roots. Place the tongue where it will keep hot. Serve with mustard sauce:

- 6 oz Italian tomato paste
- 1 teaspoon dry mustard
- 1 tablespoon sugar
- ½ teaspoon salt
- 1 tablespoon vinegar
- 1 tablespoon drained horseradish
- 1 tablespoon chopped onion, chives or fresh herbs (optional)

Thank you, Irma S. Rombauer
Joy of Cooking 1943

These Boots are made for Posting

I pulled off at Oshkosh for a quick tour when an old church, white stucco with boarded windows, caught my eye. A young woman waved when I first passed by. She was on her knees weeding a small patch of grass near the steps of the church.

Her name is Carol and she was pulling "stickers" from the grass; a pail full of the weeds sat nearby in a tangled network of green stems and leaves camouflaging spiked pods. She and her husband bought the property a year earlier which included the empty Lutheran church next door and the former parsonage which is now their home. Her efforts to open the old doors failed, so she agreed to be photographed on the front steps of the dilapidated shrine they hope to renew one day.

The train that passes through this end of Ogallala prompts my presence at the door in thirty minute intervals, the Burlington Northern returning a mile of empty cars to the Wyoming coal fields.

What does it mean? All those western boots jammed up-side-down on fence posts, miles of them in random display from the Dakotas south, an intriguing signature. How and why did it begin and whose boots? I blame the folks responsible for *Carhenge* or crop circles.

Thursday, July 11th: Spent yesterday at the word processor, and with each reading, I'm reminded of scenes recaptured. Already nodding, "… I'd nearly forgotten that."

Drove out to Ash Hollow today. Remnants of the Oregon Trail can be seen in deep ruts that cut through the plain, and from the top of a hill the winding trail is more defined, like views of Earth from space of the Great Wall, of monumental human purpose, unimaginable endurance.

Highway 92 joined the railroad for a twenty mile sweep along the north edge of *Big Mac*, Lake McConaughy, Nebraska's largest reservoir with more than a hundred miles of shore and "...at full storages, is 20 miles long, four miles wide and 142 feet deep at the dam." KOGA-AM out of Ogallala, a showcase of early fifties crooners, played the way as Glenn Miller's "In the Mood" brought a momentary aching throat, memories of my dancing daughter in Concord last summer when the streets close to traffic during Bargain Days. At its western shore, an access road ended in a grove of cottonwoods. The giant trees stood at the water's edge, thick braided roots bleached pale, an earlier water line about three feet up from the base, while smaller trees stood knee-deep at the breakwater, all of it smeared with arty strokes of pale gray, charcoal and ash.

Nebraska Time-Out: In 1972 the Cottonwood was named the official state tree, replacing the original choice, the American Elm made in 1937. The cottonwood is often associated with pioneer Nebraska, as small shoots were collected and planted on claims, many recognized as early landmarks.

Friday, July 12, North Platte, Nebraska
The Scout Motel, $21.00

Back on central time, another plateau reached. The Scout Motel sits on Rodeo Road, at the top of my financial short list, far from I-80's *bargain* offerings, and as Jim might have put it, this accommodation "wants to be described."

It had to happen. All roadside stops throughout this journey have collaged to an interesting patchwork here in North Platte. A room back in Martin, South Dakota might remind me of the one in Moose Lake south of Duluth, the entrance maybe, or the layout. Some have a fridge and a microwave; others offer in-room coffee, but no writing desk; TV, including a local channel listing, but no remote. The paradigm of affordable lodging lies here on the Platte River adjacent to a very large rail yard in Central Nebraska.

Its façade is brick, and a colorful mustard theme is first suggested by the metal yellow ochre porch chair at the turquoise door. Twin wrought iron supports hold an awning above the entry, each pole adorned with horseshoes, branding irons, and an *Aruban* bronco in full kick. On entering the room, classic seventies shag covers the floor in a tweedy mix of *French's* and *Gulden's* spattered with hints of tangerine, a subtle contrast to the fiberglass drapes. Deep brown paneling is going on from floor to ceiling.

A *Poupon* recliner sits in the corner, its *Naugahyde* (or "pleather" from plastic leather) is meticulously hemmed along its lower edge with a straight row of brass tacks, while a *Dijon* side table holds a lamp, the base of it spattered with globs of brown and white acrylic—imagine periwinkles, thousands of them clinging hideously to a peculiar ceramic shape. The *Gulden's* bedspread holds enormous tangerine flowers, while a framed print hangs above the headboard, seen in hundreds of paint-by-number works: yellow birches in the foreground, river coming at us from a distant bend, towering pines beyond and majestic snowcapped peaks against a happy blue sky, as a deer regards us with alarm from beside a fallen tree that trips the white water.

The TV cord is coiled neatly in a cardboard toilet paper tube, while the writing desk with three drawers and horseshoe pulls holds a phone and a turquoise plaster lamp. A small round table with two chairs invites us back to the kitchenette with its one-by-two rectangular sink, and the waist-high refrigerator is topped with a stainless steel sideboard beside a four-burner range—no microwave needed here—does *Budget-Lodge* out on I-80 even have a four-burner offering? Cupboards overhead hold two Styrofoam cups, this being a cash-only room; glasses wrapped in cellophane fall under the $25 to $30 credit card range.

The bathroom takes a turn of style with a better-than-average tile floor, pale gray marble, while goldfish swim playfully across a former shower curtain, custom sheared to fit the small window. The shower stall in the opposite corner is of the Spanish influence, its red tile *sunken Formica* surrounds the stall, rising a foot from the floor, topped with an arrangement of *terra-cotta-ish* stonework, a towel the color of *Gulden's* draped over the side. The walls are painted to match the spicy brown shower curtain, and Safeway grocery plastic lines the trash can.

Signed, *Mustard Flower Madame*

Saturday, July 13
Respite at Pat's Sister's

Here at the Huelfte Lodge in Gothenburg, the white cardboard sign in my room reads: "Rest here and let your soul catch up to your body," and on the mailbox outside: "Gloria."

Mind's Eye Video: young girl with three goats playing king of the mountain on a rusty oil tank; sunlight on the cornfield beyond, wide-eyed kittens in the trees watching the German shepherd chase shredded basketball rubber, bringing it over and over again to a pail of water, letting it drop, fishing it from the pail, returning it to my now soaked lap. I throw the former ball into the sun and watch him leap in slow motion, the kittens in awe of the giant dog paying them no mind, my brother's ever-frolicking Goldens come to mind. Iced tea in the shade, afternoon chat with Pat's sister in the heart of the heartland, cornfields surround us...a tour of the feedlot, hundreds of cattle, corralled and waiting, ankles in murk. Fried chicken and French green beans for dinner...coloring cutout ponies...*Für Elise* from the player piano and a dancing happy child wearing Mommy's red shoes, a swirling frock and a wide-brim hat the color of straw. Cicadas, the sound of them in the silence of dusk crackling through the air, or is it the wires, abrasive, like electricity, an indistinguishable sound. Purple clouds behind the prairie windmill. Sleep.

Will I survive the eastern trek—Memphis, Washington, Annapolis, New York, fear beginning to loom...the bridge at dawn. I need to see my children, and Arlene and Sam. Sleep. "Rest here and let your soul catch up to your body." I need to talk with Pat and Gordon back home. Make that, I need to listen to Pat and her Lucy voice. Get on with it Blockhead! And her gentle counterpart, the *Gordon voice.*

GLORIA JEAN

The Magical, Not-Making-This-Up Nebraska Moment

It was surreal, and with time the event has amplified in my mind's eye, a wonderful meditative tool when needed, my all-too-brief Nebraska moment.

I and the family attended a school recital in Gothenburg that afternoon. After the program, refreshments and social hour ended, we left the parking lot and headed home as the Union Pacific crooned its haunting lullaby through town, itself a near spiritual event. *A Summer Place* (Percy Faith, 1959) began to play on the radio, for me a perfectly timed ambiance, further igniting my state of awe as we turned on a gravel road, tires crunching, slicing through *elephant's eye* corn. While my hosts were unaware, as to them it was merely another drive home, I rode shotgun in a trance. Sunlight pressed through the clouds in shafts of white light, while a distant storm propelled in contrast across the horizon in gray chutes and flashing light. Glistening meadows ran like filmstrip through the driver's window, a dreamlike sequence: cattle at the watering trough lifting their heads to watch us pass...birds adrift like kites on the wind...dust devils dancing to Percy Faith on the dirt road ahead...violins up and down the scale...a spinning windmill in silhouette against the lowering sun...the mile-long howl of a freight train...rapture...over too soon.

Sunday morning we attended the Evangelical Church found at the end of more gravel byways, always, always among fields of corn. Adult Sunday school prior to the church service, a dozen of us seated around a table, smiling reaffirmation, praising God for my visit. That day's lesson: "All great civilizations fell when immorality reigned... Israel remains." Same-sex marriages and the like, love, angst, pop music—disdain for that world beyond the corn.

A solemn young man—Randy Travis without the smile— sat silently across the table, intense, from the Amish underground maybe, staring at his Bible, no words to say, no beaming, nodding head or glowing face like the others with each affirmation of God's glorious earth. Lily Tomlin got her characters out here—Ernestine lives with the Church Lady. But what's *his* story? I need to know his story. What's he getting out of coming to this room? My earnest face masked a bit of inner coaching:

You're too damn young to look like that! Swallow some Jack Daniels upside the head for cryin' out loud and stop that pickup! Let's hear the Stones on this gravel road, guy! C'mon! Don't go to your grave in that condition!

Thank you, Dr. Ruth!

CHAPTER 26

Kansas

July 16 to 18, Hays, Kansas
The General Hays Inn, $62.78

"The John Dunbar Theme" from *Dances with Wolves* is played with each pass of Old Fort Hays, its giant stone bison at the crest of the hill, turned slightly, steadfast to the hot breath of the prairie. Across the highway, a small herd stood corralled on the campus of Hays State University, the bull towering over his small family, a picture perfect ensemble for the haunting melody. My inner groupie imagined Kevin Costner at random street corners.

The General Hays Motel will be remembered for its efficient air cooling; in a word: refrigeration, but the price was right for a three-day hitch. Yesterday a drive through the town of Russell, Kansas, home of Senator Robert Dole, and farther along, my response to a compelling brochure, an invitation to the *Garden of Eden* up in Lucas.

In 1907 at the age of sixty-four, Civil War Veteran Samuel Dinsmoor, retired schoolteacher, artist, farmer, and populist politician, began work on his *Cabin Home and Garden of Eden*. For twenty-two years he fashioned 113 tons of cement along with tons of limestone into his unique "log" cabin, surrounded by some two hundred concrete sculptures reflecting his religious convictions and belief in the populist movement; think Dr. Seuss meets Americana. It was noted that while he was building and creating, locals tried to run him out of town, but decades later the *Garden of Eden* would become the town's main attraction, world-renowned for one of the most fascinating and bizarre sculpture gardens in the world. Dinsmoor also built a mausoleum to house his mummified remains, and today Lucas is known as the Grassroots Art Capital of Kansas.

> "If you're hanging around with nothing to do, and the zoo is closed, come over to the Senate. You'll get the same kind of feeling and you won't have to pay."
>
> —US Senator Robert J. "Bob" Dole,
> Rep., Kansas

Friday, July 19, Dodge City, Kansas
The Astro Motel, $33.75

Blew into Dodge on US Highway 50/56 and "experienced" a brief stopover at its *Cattle Feedlot Overlook*, a brown-on-brown patchwork of corrals, hundreds of doomed cattle congregated in square enclosures, a checkerboard, too many to count because "it's what's for dinner."

Dodge City, Kansas, could be compared to Plymouth Plantation in the *Bay State*, a tidy recreation of the past. Boot Hill included a corner of the original plot with a neat stone walkway among wooden slabs bearing the names of a few. Paid for a self-guided tour through *Old Dodge* set apart from the downtown area.

Chose the Astro Motel ($33.75), a clean corner away from it all to witness opening ceremonies of the Olympics in Atlanta, *The Centennial Games*. The spectacle begins with a photo montage and the voice of Neil Diamond, "Coming to America." Then trumpets, as the world churns—TWA Flight 800 entombed off Long Island.

Oklahoma

Saturday, July 20, Woodward, Oklahoma
Sleepy Hollow Motel, $27.63

There is no weather today. Expression has withered here on the plains, Kansas left behind, no sunflower fields to be seen—interesting response from a sampling of natives when asked about their state blossom, one of them a staff member at the Tourist Center back in Hays. None could answer the question. "Seen them out toward Wichita, I think…this would certainly be the time of year…maybe west of here."

The extremely polite traffic cop here in Woodward apologized for asking that I reroute myself through town. The parade was about to begin, led by politicians in convertibles cloaked in red, white, and blue, and horse-drawn carriages getting into place along the street. It's Rodeo weekend here, traffic factor high—it and the thermometer's ninety-seven degrees. "Dalmatian Horse" with an antique fire wagon was a no show.

The Sleepy Hollow Motel offers relative luxury for the price than was found in Custer, South Dakota, on the fourth of July—a queen-size bed, the first one so far, and a spacious cool room in which to catch up on the Olympics. Dare I put this in writing: that the opening ceremonies last night were a trifle excessive. The Greek temple, Olympians backlit would have done it, and Mr. Ali's lighting of the torch was awe-inspiring, but the rest of it tedious. There were giant gossamer moths and antebellum puppets, excessive costuming and a hundred bursts of firepower. My inner child went back to the fifties and the *Ice Follies at Rhode Island Auditorium in Providence.* This production reminds me of a Super Bowl halftime show, how to top the last one. I'm gettin' old, apparently. Is this what *jaded* means? Gladys Knight was stunning, however. And by the way, one clear theme song would do it, one lone runner approaching the great lamp. There's glory in the power of one; leave 'em wanting more, not falling asleep only to miss the damn entrance of Team USA!

I've avoided this journal over the past week, each day lacking the promise of a great moment, just a different stretch of road, while the heat stifles any urge for adventure, my room a hot flash-free oasis. Tomorrow my long ago New England friends, relocated to "Okie City."

July 21 to 25, Oklahoma City

Finding suburban Piedmont presented no problem! Cocky New England driver decides to find Northridge Lane through superhuman sense of direction. An hour later, sick of daze-driving, having passed the same dead armadillo twice, I asked for directions and found the center of town from which to call.

I was no longer behind the wheel, as we shared the drama of Jackie and Dave's *home on the range* neighborhood. It was a thrilling opening night event, this land of the great wind, as a massive red cloud pushed to the east with fork lightning in staccato mile high streaks. Punishing gusts bullied the nervous horses next door, riding fringes of the passing gale like a carousel in their western backyard.

Enjoying auto tours around Oklahoma neighborhoods, a passenger this time, relishing the mental respite, no maps, no eye on the roadside for tonight's lodging, only the sweep of ranches, herds of cattle, black, brown, gray marble and butterscotch watching us pass. Limousin Cattle, the *butterscotches*, are a prized breed, more commonly raised on so-called *Cadillac Ranches* like the one we passed on the way out of town, an immaculately groomed brick mansion centered at the top of a slope, its cupola rising above like Churchill Downs, an extraordinary setting.

Dinner at *The Wilds,* a local catfish hatchery, miles from any main road. There was a small zoo on the grounds with goats waiting by the corn dispensers, along with an assortment of ducks. Two coyotes pace with exhausting repetition, penned in a tiny stifling world.

We drove along old Route 66, and in the tiny town of Chandler toured a remarkable place: *The Museum of Prairie Life,* a large two-story block building with rooms arranged and presented in their own time: a schoolroom, doctor's office, kitchen, bedroom, quilting racks, printing presses, a telephone operator's station, barbed wire displays, most exhibits hands-on except for fragile items that were roped off. In Guthrie, a trolley ride passed through a virtual museum of turn of the century architecture: prairie bungalows, Queen Anne Mansions, *painted ladies,* colonial revival homes and Oklahoma's first capitol building. In 1910, Oklahoma's newly established state government held an election to decide where the capitol should be located and the state seal was moved from Guthrie to Oklahoma City.

The Human Link

We walk in silence, alone at once in quiet sorrow as the sun sinks beyond Oklahoma City's broken heart. The downtown, only a block away, is forgotten, silent. My throat aches, eyes filled with tears. In another time and place this would be called a chain-link fence, but here in the looming shadow of Timothy McVeigh, it cuts across the block like callous sutures through a jagged wound, woven end to end in a patchwork of ribbons, flowers, notes, and tributes, a sad human tapestry. There are teddy bears, Indian jewelry, hats, T-shirts and photos, so many families, children laughing, smiles reaching from the fence, a happier time, life as they knew it forever gone. Chiseled ridges of the bombed-out building stand in jagged stone parameters to the mute display—168 souls.

The Dead

Food seems offered at every turn—barbecue, smoked sausage, and ribs. I need to get back on line. My family history of clogged arteries is a continued haunt here in beef and gravy world. Perhaps it was the Murrah Building, revisiting its horror that prompts my death dreams. Last night it was Jim, unsettling in the seeming reality of his presence in the room, seated at the foot of my bed. We had a conversation, but I'm unable to recall its content. Another was an uncle who died back in the seventies. Why do they visit me now? Am I not destined to complete this trek? The Brooklyn Bridge at dawn has become a menace of shadows, like the earlier nightmare months ago, the ghastly presence on a darkened roof staring through me before the mindless kill. Will it be Memphis, or will it happen in Annapolis when I visit Chip's grave—a distracting, rustling shroud, this hesitation.

*****

Thursday, July 25, Eufaula, Oklahoma
The Loyal Inn, $32.35

Jackie and Dave: I survived my Oklahoma City exit with little problem, only one impatient horn blower. I'm located at the Loyal Inn in Eufaula Lake 125 miles east and will head through the Jack Ford Mountain area tomorrow—mountain? Really? I need to express once more how much I appreciated your "cheap motel." Hadn't realized how much a home away from home was needed till I'd been with you a while having real conversations with dear friends. If I hadn't been so wary of losing my place again, I might have taken one last spin past the cow in the pond photo op but lacked confidence in light of that first day's dead armadillo tour.

As the weeks pass, I'm beginning to relish the memory of certain places and people along the way. It seems to take a week or so for one sequence or another to resurface, usually after the film is developed, or that night's TV news of softball-size hail that passed through my former town. I'm remembering our time in your garage beholding the great red cloud passing in the distance. For the wonderful food, sociable cat, room and board, auto tours and museums, I thank you immensely. Hope that now I've departed you won't suffer a dreadful prairie outburst.

The armadillo lives inside
A corrugated plated hide
Below the border this useful creature
Of tidy kitchens is a feature
For housewives use an armadillo
To scour their pots, instead of Brillo

—Ogden Nash

Brillo, as you might have guessed,
Is a steel wool pad like SOS

—Gloria Jean

Friday/Saturday, July 26 to 27, Hugo, Oklahoma
The Village Inn, $63.04

On certain stretches of road, mental reruns surface. Today it was people, and there's a novel along the road, a bittersweet recollection. I on the fringe feel an immunity to certain prisons, having survived the bottom of the black well with no light at the top, no one to end it, until it ended. I'm alone, not lonely, no need for a "companion," an awful marker for the golden years. *Vagabond Chic* hits the road at fifty-something, three months alone.

Youth, young love, at times still seems like the recent past. Dave was a sailor on the USS Essex based at Quonset Point. Jackie was pregnant with their first child. They lived in navy housing; he was on a cruise when the Thresher went down in 1963. We were twenty somethings with wedding presents to adorn our frugally arranged apartments, husbands going to school or getting out of the service, the first baby, moving on. Twenty-five years pass, and it seems to have vanished in the steam of Oklahoma.

What's to come in Texas with Renee and Lanny? Another navy couple from 1968, both from Texas, he a Seabee doing a hitch in Vietnam, she age eighteen, living with Mike and me for those eight months, working at URI in the Football Office. Every football coach, football player and PhysEd major had eyes for the *yellow rose*. She was away from home for the first time in her life, swept up in the adulation; surely that marriage was doomed, but the navy hitch ended, Mike and I moved to New Hampshire, and soon after, they returned to Texas. They're still together; Mike and I didn't make it.

I'm headed for Texas, my last month out, and while I don't want this to end, long to squeeze hands at home, Sam and Arlene's, as Sam's chest twinges cause anxieties all around, like a stone in the pond. I'd head home tomorrow if need be. And Michele's job search. I knelt at the bed last night with the antique Bible, praying for her placement where I know she'll shine in the world of eldercare, an arena inherently hers. Like the path of this journey, I'm convinced she's divinely guided.

Hiked through another *middle of nowhere* today on a side road out of the public park at Lake Hugo, a footpath through dense woods, eerily reminiscent of Civil War diaries, inner terrors of the soldier child pushing through the undergrowth, stifling humidity, and the unrelenting drone of insects, unseen, piercing the brain laser-like. A swinging footbridge carried my distractions across a murky brown creek, lush vines hanging drenched from the trees, creeping across rotted trunks, truly alone on a spongy green viaduct. A camera couldn't have brought it home: sizzling heat, the grinding screech of cicadas, shafts of sunlight, and near-visible steam. I could leave this life here and never be found.

CHAPTER 28

Texas

This has all become an odyssey among critters. A committee of twelve grazed near the roadside. Bright sun and a soft breeze rustled tall grasses along the fence, showcasing horses of many colors. While most of them continued to graze, a few glanced with polite interest while a chestnut mare stood at the fence discouraging others from sharing the visit. Her soft nose brushed my arm, later a scan of my cheek, and when I stepped aside to photograph the others, horse whiskers rustled against my ear. The soft, hollow roar of her nostrils nudged for a glimpse through the lens. She had no distinctive markings except for the nicks and scratches that come with virtual horseplay. Her face studied mine with short measured sniffs and tubular hollow sighs as the velvet nose passed across my face. Welcome to Texas, Gloria Jean!

Sunday, July 28, Sulphur Springs, Texas
The Royal Inn, $32.35

The Laundromat is adorned along its upper wall with posters from the thirties and forties, tin rectangles in muted colors, spaced along the wall above the dryers—Drink Brownie in Bottles 5 cents, KO Your Thirst With KAYO, Old Abe Cigars, For the People! 25 cents, Missouri Pacific Lines, Old Gold Cigarettes.

Ceiling fans move slightly cool air, and I in my baggy pants and T-shirt feel crudely dressed compared to the family that just entered, coming from church I would guess, carrying five heaping baskets of laundry. The mother and three young girls wear dresses and stockings; the two younger girls in white lace and patent leather shoes; the older girl, a teen with long black hair tied back with red ribbon, is wearing a red print dress, stockings, and short white heels. Dad wears a white shirt, buttoned at the neck, with a bolo tie, boots, and a western hat. Today's temp is ninety-eight degrees. How do people do it out here? New Hampshire folk are immobilized when, for several days in July, ninety-degree heat is headline news. Stay inside, the sky is falling. And have I even mentioned hot flashes?

Two young men sit on a bench by the window sipping Cokes, laughing between them, pointing to a vehicle parked outside. Young dudes talking cars, most likely my hot Geo, the seductive color of taupe. Aside from the bombing of Atlanta's Olympic Park, a scan of the newspaper confirms the heat: today, sun ninety-eight degrees, (it bears repeating), Monday, sun ninety-six degrees, Tuesday, sun... Wednesday, mostly sun. The laundry family fill six washers, blankets, spreads, lights, and colors—no woven labels that I could see—and all the while Mother was soothing the fussing young lady in white lace, wishing to play elsewhere, while my efforts at conversation, or rather, my limitations, fail to change her mood.

Hindsight: Say what you mean; mean what you say. Next time, *learn* Spanish!

Renee waits just south of here for our reunion tomorrow in the tiny town of Emory. Twenty-eight years spent, we have grown children, vastly different lives, the *Reb* and the *Yankee* with a lifetime to tell. Am I there yet? When will I get there? What will she look like? Her voice sounds the same. I was twenty-seven then, and she eighteen back in '68, working girls in the boys' gym at URI, she in the football office and I for the athletic director, a first job that spoiled me for all others to come. College athletics behind the scenes—Bobby Knight calling from West Point, Red Auerbach coming in tomorrow, Bob Cousy the coach at Boston College; the PC game always a sellout, their players the likes of John Thompson, Georgetown's future coach, and Billy Flynn, the mayor of Boston and future ambassador to the Vatican, Len Wilkins et cetera, et cetera, Julius Irving just another

UMass *Red Man*. Oh, and the Pittsburgh Steelers' summer training camp in our backyard. I hear the hypnotic rhythm of their cleats each day marching the halls, headed for practice—pre-Bradshaw, I should point out. But here's the memory I'm saving for *The Home* one day: our spontaneous campus dining room chorus honoring Oklahoma's favorite son, Steelers defensive back and shoulda-been-a-movie-star, Clendon Thomas. It sings through my mind at least once a year, *just yesterday,* the entire cafeteria surging, voices swelling *O-K-L-A-H-O-M-A Oak-a-luh-HOME-ma! Yeow!* Clendon Thomas's gracious smile lit the room—*hunk* status easily on par with Gordon MacRae.

It was Renee's first time-out of Texas, and Lanny's Seabee hitch would be spent in Vietnam for eight months—the sixties, America's national tailspin. The war in Vietnam, Martin Luther King and Robert Kennedy, Malcolm X and Medgar Evers all added to the sad parade headed by JFK. *Laugh-In* on TV, flower children, *The Graduate* and *Bonnie & Clyde*, Gene Hackman's early rising star. We followed the Barrow gang for a least three sittings—that's three trips to a movie theater.

Tomorrow I'll pull into town and call her from the courthouse square as instructed. What have we come to since 1968? She says she's overweight, so am I. What are the pages between? And what's the cattle business like? There's a lot to be learned, and pictures, many more pictures of cattle, horses, and Renee, foxy sixties chick, straight out of *Laugh-In's* party scene, Goldie Hawn's brunette double hits middle age. Are we there yet?

I'm reminded that I've been in this area before. It was early June 1968 when Renee received word that her cousin Wendell had "died in a wreck." The news for her was devastating, and I accompanied her sad return home for the funeral. If I remember correctly, we stayed in her grandmother's house, the place where Renee and Lanny now reside.

Much of that time has faded from memory, except for the open casket placed in the living room and the frequent arrival of grieving friends and family paying their respects, a first such practice in my distant New England experience. My guest room across the hall offered its own asides, what with coyotes howling and peacocks screaming in the night. Didn't know peacocks sounded like that. Mocking? They never seemed to shut up, although my fitful state of slumber might have inflated five minutes to five or six hours. Grow up, Gloria, you're twenty-seven. Wendell sleeps peacefully in the living room; nothing to see here. Daylight soon.

Our last night in Texas was spent at the Executive Inn in Dallas to ensure connection with our early flight the next morning. Renee's uncle drove us through the downtown along Elm Street, Dealey Plaza, the School Book Depository, and the infamous grassy knoll. Dinner at a steak house included my first taste of Rocky Mountain oysters: amusing for them, another *first* for me. Yep, calf testicles. No, really, but this was not revealed, of course, until they were fully consumed by me. Well, the joke's on them. I happen to love scallops, and Rocky Mountain oysters closely resembles the flavor of scallops—if one doesn't dwell upon what is being eaten!

Early to bed, set the clock radio, as November 22, 1963, lingers toward sleep.

The clock radio that morning was frantic with steady urgent chatter. My state of grog was heavy, still dreaming it seemed, as I kept hearing "assassinated" and "Kennedy." I was reliving 1963. But my awakening became surreal when the unimaginable reality was understood: another Kennedy shot, this one Robert, this time in Los Angeles. But that was then.

Eureka! It's high noon, and I've found Prairie Rose here in the tiny, slow-roasted town of Emory, Texas—water tower, main street, the shaded court house, hot Texas afternoon, the scene of our loud reunion to come, a momentary ruckus sure to interrupt the midday lull. I placed the call and waited for her car to roar into town, a big ol' Texas car, like a rowdy tornado, its own dust bowl. Not even sure what kind of car it was, something out of the seventies. She parked sideways in front of the courthouse and flew from its front seat, the door hanging open. Glo! She yelped. Can't type *Glo,* the way she would shriek the name. Lots of rowdy behavior, like those winners on *The Price Is Right,* no prissy New England reserve here in Texas! Let the reruns begin. It'll take us a few sundowns to get these nearly thirty years put to rest. God, would you please just turn the heat down!

Tuesday July 30, Emory Livestock Auction

Leland Calverley, my cattle auction professor, age eleven of Wills Point, Texas, solved all the mysteries of the auction barn, all the questions dragged along since Miles City, watching cattle arrive in truckloads, led to a nearby barn, the mystery sound, steel slamming together in measured intervals, horsemen riding to and fro, their hats in shadows against the light of the open corral beyond, back and forth in silhouette, whistling, prodding over the low bellow of annoyed cattle. I'd guess it was because of that heavy THWACK! Was it a scale, some kind of slamming door, what?

We had walked through the corrals looking at livestock, small herds waiting in pens, or arriving in semis, unloaded into vacant lots, all appearing accustomed to the murk and baking sun, waiting for something. Inside the barn we strolled a catwalk above the animals, an assortment of goats, horses and cattle—Brahmans, Limousin, and Charolais; calves, steers, boney seniors, and enormous bulls waiting backstage, ready for a walk-on. This time I was with *insiders*. Renee walked me through it. Livestock auctions are held here twice a week and her husband Lanny runs the concession throughout the long day and into the night, a grueling repetitious schedule, reminding me of our convenience store grind back in the eighties.

Young Calverley spotted my camera. He and his mother were browsing the livestock below, shopping for a "kid's horse" she said. He asked if I was "…a phro…afratogafur." I told him about my trip west and curiosity about the process. The lesson began. Had I ever seen the "squayshew?" (*I tell you what! Them dang' ol Texas accents!*)

"The what?" "The *SQUAY*shew." "How do you spell that?" He stammered a minute. "Well, can you spell 'squeeze'? Then spell 'shoot'." *That* squeeze chute! *That thwack!*

The steel frame opens at both ends to receive the unsuspecting animal for a series of, uh, internal procedures. The pushing and prodding and whistling leads them through a corral, as each one is directed into the chute which then secures the critter with a loud THWACK, allowing little mobility as the technicians do their work. The teeth are examined for age, the ear pressed with a metal tag. Blood is drawn and the back end is examined by a vet wearing a plastic glove the length of his arm who palpates for pregnancy—*that* animal husbandry. The bovine is stamped, temporarily branded with a paste-like chalk: T for tested, V for vaccinated, 3 for three years old and 4 for four months pregnant; SS for short and stout (age not known); Y for yearling or H for heifer (or something like that, not sure I got it all right). A heifer is a young cow over one year old that has not produced a calf.

I photographed my professor outside, and he obliged my request to pick a Texas stone from the ground for Joey Holland, age ten, back in Rhode Island. The young boy passed it to me with a handshake, the stone between our hands, a great big Texas moment!

Inside, the amphitheater houses the auction arena, in another time and place and with a whole lot of imagination, Sotheby's maybe, except for the odor and the monotone humana-humana drone of the auctioneer and quick motions of his hand with each bid as his side-kick scans the room to catch sight of a raised card, another number called—humana, humana, sixty, humana, sixty-five. An unexpected moment of silence occurs when one cow enters the arena before her time. There is silence as she wanders to the fenceline and seems to scan the audience for a familiar face, causing some stifled laughter, then continuation of the bidding. Hummana-hummana. Two men to the right of the auctioneer, open and close gates for each entrance or exit, jumping behind steel barricades to avoid kicks or an occasional angry charge as the animal enters, turns, stands and whirls in confusion amid the hummana beat. My near hypnosis was interrupted when the auctioneer's words finally reached me: "Now,

Gloria, wouldn't you like to take a few of these beautiful critters back to New Hampshire with you?" Hummana hummana hummana. Lanny-behind-the-scenes is more a comedian than I remembered. A hundred western hats turned my way to smile.

Thursday, August 1

One more time, this has been an odyssey among critters—horses, cattle, moose, bison, various cats, and beginning in Oklahoma, an assortment of armadillos, usually cracked like walnuts on the roadside. I did slow down for a live one that crossed the road ahead, its toes tapping the pavement as if wearing tiny high heeled shoes.

Here in Texas, I've befriended a Chihuahua, a rusty shorthair, the color of Limousin cattle, a real charmer—I, having owned two St. Bernards, beguiled by a footnote. Known in these parts as "Duke," he has erect pointed ears, liquid brown eyes, and the snout of a red fox with fine black whiskers. He moves in quick, darting jabs like a windup toy and howls pathetically when left in a room alone, nuzzling for comfort like a quivering kitten, a passable stand-in, I think, for Golda Meow who waits back east, please God, for the return of her devoted, *not forgotten* servant.

Today was time spent with goats, Boer Goats, residing with a satellite dish in the back pasture, a herd of about twenty-eight before the babies arrive, a South African breed, larger and stockier than most, white with the trademark brown head. We wandered among them while Duke sat on the other side of the fence. Apparently his earlier quarrel with a nanny hadn't gone his way, so he chose to wait it out on less confrontational ground, howling his low self-esteem across the yard. Just yesterday the family cat named Brutus gave him the *what-for*, and the few cattle in a nearby pasture offer little or no response to his herding techniques, although I did notice one of them politely lower its head to the dog: *"Kinda teeny for a big feller, ain't cha?"*

My son's call this morning shot me with dread; the echo of his one-word "Mum," its controlled hoarseness, prepared the way for bad news. Zachary, the dog of his childhood, his companion through heartache and joy, had to go to sleep, an inconsolable event for my twenty-four year old trying to hold it together, impossible to handle across the wires half a country away. I encouraged him to have a good wail and to be there for his father who was probably in worse emotional shape.

This mood held me in a net today, stirring my fringes of concern for helpless *dumb* animals, like the cattle baking in mud outside the auction barn. During the sale, one bedraggled cow fell to her knees in the arena, bawling her exhaustion while the men tried to whack her rear into a standing position. She was finally encouraged through gates into the area beyond, her destiny most likely hastened.

And the goat this afternoon, a nanny that had pushed her head through a square of wire fencing, now locked in place by her horns. She'd been standing there for most of the day, helpless to remove herself. Renee assured me that Lanny would set her out tonight after he gets home. Had the goat barbecued there all day in triple-digit heat? The mental picture of her predicament interrupted more as the hours passed. It could be well into the night before he gets here. I mentally walked myself through the process: straddle the goat, grab both horns, then twist her head sideways and back through the wire square, a *Texas* accomplishment, my chance at it. *Ask for the chance to try. No, just do it. Set the nanny free!*

She was stronger than we—than I—had imagined. Not a small goat, fighting our attempts at tilting her head to the side and backward through the square, pushing her horns, and my wrists against the wire. Renee finally got it done. My mind could think of other things now. This mood must be shaken. What's causing the downhill slide? Must be the stifling humidity. Hot flashes? You want hot flashes? In Texas, I'm the goddamn queen of hot flashes!

Writing from the soul needs to continue. A nagging feeling of dread grabbed my ankle back in Oklahoma in dreams of those who've gone before, and it seemed to break the spell. The exhilaration that flung my spirit to other destinies seems gone, no longer the wonder. What was it? What's going to happen? The drive through northeastern mazes is intimidating. Was it too long an agenda? Am I simply tired? Too old? A curtain of mist now; what's to come? It's been my question all along. What's to come of this? Decompression rapid.

> "My own journey started long before I left, and was over before I returned. I know exactly where and when it was over. Near Abingdon, in the dogleg of Virginia, at four o'clock of a windy afternoon, without warning or good-by or kiss my foot, my journey went away and left me stranded far from home. I tried to call it back, to catch it up—a foolish and hopeless matter, because it was definitely and permanently over and finished..."

—John Steinbeck, *Travels with Charley: In Search of America*

*****

Zachary Hound
Enjoyed fishing, Frisbees
Pittsfield, NH, August 1996

Zack was a tall *Somewhat Irish Wolfhound*, a lanky elegant gentleman, proud of his slate gray curls. In the spring, when first clipped of his winter coat, he appeared embarrassed, uncomfortable with the sudden weight loss. His distinguished expression was accented with moveable brush eyebrows that shifted in different directions as he scanned the landscape (or the kitchen), and his long legs carried him across the land with agile grace.

He enjoyed hunting, fishing, and leaping for Frisbees. He liked to spend time at the edge of a backyard stream, scanning its gravel floor until the unfortunate quarry, usually a frog, was lifted from the water, its legs hanging from the dog's teeth, dripping, sparkling in sunlight, an arresting image.

In canine circles, Hound's conversational skill was unparalleled. Positioned at the door, seizing one's eye contact while thrashing his tail against the wood in the rhythm of a bass drum, his jaws seemed to unhinge, forming gnarled contortions, howling numerous high pitched syllables in the style of Reba McIntyre.

Aside from his human family, he is survived by his companion, a Lhasa Apso named Dreyfus, the walking bedroom slipper who shared his space.

*****

The unsettling death dream back in Oklahoma manifested itself yesterday. "Sam didn't make it," were Karen's words from Rhode Island. "The doctor can't explain it, the surgery had gone so well. He died in the recovery room."

We had spoken on the phone two days earlier when I called him at the hospital. The fear in his voice echoes now in haunting phrases. He was facing heart surgery and would be in "good shape" after it was over, ready to do "whatever it takes." He sounded fragile, my Aunt Sam, the big ol' boy from Exeter who had a million stories to tell of growing up on the farm and the *early to bed, early to rise* hardscrabble life he lived. Back in the fifties and sixties he was master of the "Exeter Town Farm" where he kept a herd of forty-five milk cows.

My impression of him was always of stubborn toughness, so it struck me when he spoke once of leaving for Fort Dix as a young man—so simply stated and with no apology—his acute fear of getting on that train in 1943. He and Arlene married later in life, and it became comic practice when introducing them to say, "This is my aunt, Arlene," and "this is my Aunt Sam" somehow fell into place. He was self-employed, an excavating contractor, and it's impossible to picture him without a pipe balanced in his teeth, operating the heavy equipment that filled his garage—bulldozers, dump trucks, and backhoes. He loved to tell jokes, usually after a few swigs, and had a repertoire of poems, including an epic saga of what seemed like fifty verses, all recited from memory, the colorful tale of an old man living in the back woods. How I'd love to retrieve that Homeric yarn for all time, but that too is gone.

"Sam didn't make it" were my cousin's words.

CHAPTER 29

Homeward

Dawn's humidity wrapped me in its weight while night sounds were still in rhythm as the household slept—our good-byes had been covered last night. I headed toward sunrise across Lake Fork, streaked like a thin sheet of tarnished steel, its dead trees hovering in ghostly formation on flat silver water. Pickups pulled out of the service station with boats in tow, and the sun seemed to stall in its upward trudge, a translucent luminous peach. I and the Geo were Rhode Island bound.

It's Sunday morning and gospel music dominates the airwaves as I cross into Arkansas for a brief stop in Hope, the birthplace of William Jefferson Clinton. It was to have been my next destination from which to watch the Democratic Convention. Picked a rock from McDonald's parking lot for Joey's collection, and later was surprised to find myself in Missouri's boot heel before a quick pass into Tennessee.

Missouri Time-Out

According to one story, the boot heel was added because a certain Missourian wanted to remain in the state "as he had heard it was so sickly in Arkansas, full of bears and panthers and copperhead snakes, so it ain't safe for civilized people to stay there overnight even."

Sunday, August 4
Mayfield Super 8, Mayfield, Kentucky—$50.00

So this is it. Vagabond Chic's plan got itself done in Texas. Drove northeast through the state of Arkansas and crossed the Mississippi, ending up here at the west end of Kentucky, 558 miles later, the same tomorrow, all focus shifted home.

No Memphis, no Beale Street or Graceland. Even worse, on another level, my long-anticipated homage to Chip in Annapolis. It simply can't happen right now—farther along, old friend, farther along. Always about the music was Chip Sayres, class of sixty-one, the Everly Brothers' *Songs Our Daddy Taught Us,* his gift to me decades ago. Which song might I have chosen to recall at his grave? Still thinking—probably "Barbara Allen." At Vietnam's Wall, a tribute to the late Richard Bishop also *might have been.* And I'll say it now: walking Brooklyn's Bridge at sunrise seemed to intimidate my plan from the beginning, often a startling apparition across the miles, like a bully waiting at the end of the hall. In a word: trepidation; oh let's just say it: fear! In my soul, was it looming, or simply awaiting my courageous dawn stroll? How might that have gone, really? Is vagrancy an official crime? Whatever happened to hobos? Or, would I be seen as a wacky person—"Apple Annie," trudging alone in the shadows toward Brooklyn? Would NYPD deliver me to Bellevue or toss me in the slammer, mug shot, bad hair, and all? Where would I leave my car? What would Wilfred do? *Well, he wouldn't be walking, Gloria Jean. He'd be driving, fool! It's not safe to walk alone at night in New York City!*

Orient Point on Long Island where Mr. Steinbeck's *travels* began was to be the final passage, where the ferry would carry me to Rhode Island, back to the embrace of my Hathaway family. I've imagined them waving from the dock as the ferry pulls into Pt. Judith, cheering my arrival—my coming home, three insulators in tow, and twenty-three rocks for Joey Holland's remarkable show and tell.

*****

Flashback, 1957

We were teenagers in the fifties, living the *Happy Days* dream in Quonset Manor, Rhode Island's postwar "Levittown," mostly navy families with a few Rhode Island natives mixed in. King Phillip Drive and connecting streets were lined with small two bedroom Cape Cod houses with colorful front doors and matching shutters, some with a garage, some with dormers, others not. Mike lived next door. He was the paperboy who toted a transistor radio on his bicycle, known for crooning "Little Darlin'" with The Drifters in fine falsetto—*fine* by me, as I was the one with the crush. Chip, Jack, and my best friend Kay lived across the circle, a rotary of giant white pines, the focal point of our teenage joys and woes, such as the passing of Buddy Holly in February 1959. All of it was played to the tune of jets roaring, low and loud out of the base. Each summer, when the Blue Angels did their show at the Navy Relief Carnival, two, sometimes four at a time, would screech overhead in tight formation, as if woven together, seemingly inches above the circle, rattling windows, shuddering roofs, the approach a sudden breathtaking squeal, shooting for the base three miles east.

At night we listened to Wolfman Jack, Alan Freed—*WINS WINS WINS NY*—Bill Haley, Elvis, Chuck Berry, and Little Richard. My friend Bobbi lived in Plantations Park across the pond—more Cape Cods along winding streets. She played ukulele and we loved singing all things Everly. She was Phil, I was Don; we were never discovered, though. "*500 Miles*" was another favorite.

Most of the moms in Quonset Manor were homemakers, while the dads had something to do with the navy. Eisenhower was president and Sputnik was both intriguing and alarming, but not to worry, there were bomb shelters—somewhere—and in school, our desks would protect us. We'd be fine.

Chip was a sunny blond guy with a great smile like Tab Hunter, and he would be my friend forever. Mike, the boy next door, was my future husband and father of our children, but Chip in my heart, was my forever friend whom I'd see again one day. There was a six-year-old in our neighborhood nicknamed Gus—or "Guth," as he would say it through missing front teeth. His best effort at saying Gloria was *GLAWgee*. "Hi *GLAWgee*," he would singsong. "Is that your boyfriend, *GLAWgee?*" He had an interesting way of calling my dog, Puff, the urgent declaration coming out like so: "Pus is looth! Pus is looth!" "G'bye Glawgeee...are ya gonna kiss him, Glawgeee?" So Chip's nickname for me was inevitable, and it echoed across the circle or through the corridors at school, and now, ever in my memory. Often he would stick his head inside his locker, and *GLAWgeeeeeeee* would reverberate to the next town.

Thirty years later, those summer nights drifted through the memory like a canister of film that's run its time as the projector snaps in rhythm to announce the end. But it seemed to haunt me as I tried over and over to make sense of it, to place it in context, and not in the *Twilight Zone*. This sort of thing doesn't really happen. I can't remember when exactly, but I awoke suddenly, and the first thought to reach me was of Chip, his voice echoing from a locker—*GLAWgee! GLAWgeeeeeee!* I smiled at the memory, but at the same time it was unsettling. *GLAWgee!* Hadn't heard that word in thirty years. Last time we knew, he was living in Maryland, an engineer with NASA. *GLAWgee!* It hung in the air for a week or two. I thought about trying to find him. But my daughter put an end to Chip Sayres with an innocent passing remark, a second thought as we were about to end a phone chat. It struck me like a punch. "Oh, Gram said to be sure and let you know that Chip died...suddenly...heart attack, I think...sailing off Annapolis." She heard it from his mother. "Chip died."

*****

Tuesday, August 6
Motel 6, Bradford, Connecticut—$44.79

I'm back in New England, 1583 miles from Emory, Texas, my last night on the *Vagabond Trail*. The muffler is drooping, starting to roar, might be disconnected, so I'll pray for a helpful, smiling repairman tomorrow who waits across the street.

Trying to prepare myself for reentry, not quite sure what to expect. My mind churns for a chance to compile these pages. How will it read to others? Would it inspire anyone else to brave the unknown in later years? Waiting for the stories to settle, for the words to weave. Many people to thank. Feeling worn down. Damn muffler!

Friday, August 16th

This day would have brought about a ceremonious crossing into Memphis, of crossing the bridge into Graceland. I *am* in Graceland of a sort, Elm Grove Cemetery in Allenton, Rhode Island, at the grave of Stephen Wilfred Hathaway, the  insulator placed and a photograph taken for Mr. Patrick at the Hathaway Bar back in Montana.

When is it going to crash? My *self* waits, as outside a gate, two months of odyssey, of pilgrimage. Where was my Oz? Three or more years of planning, daily spells of spinning the web, a fire that consumed me, of interest to only a few, but it still burned and I brought it about. It happened, and now this gateway to cross. Here, parked in a cemetery, the trance evaporates in fading puffs. I too may disintegrate, stifling emotion, afraid of what lies ahead.

"How's your day, ma'am?" Where to now, *ma'am?*

Signed, *Fat Lady Singing*
Odometer: *70,781*

August 1996

Little is said among this Rhode Island family about my *epic* journey. Visions of it filtered in glimpses throughout the funeral, of settling things, ushering Arlene, the widow, my mother, into her own days to come. Sam didn't choose his demise or the odyssey's abrupt end. This too was part of the destiny, deeper reasoning known only to the Master Weaver, "Farther along, I'll understand why."

Do I miss it? Did I want it to end anyway? Dread had been building, of navigating the cluttered cities back east, finding Brooklyn and the sail across Long Island Sound.

Get home. Write it down.

*****

Readjusting All Over Again, Yogi

Golda Meow's return home was of great concern. How would my Queen of the House take to another upheaval? Convinced I'd have to keep her indoors for at least a week or two, pending her reacquaintment, I carried my cat into the house, her weight shifting within the awful box. I lowered it to the floor in the entry hall and unhinged the top. She sprang from the chariot as expected, strolled to her special dining area in the kitchen, pausing for a rub against the stereo speaker placed along the way, the one with the worn spot covered with her strawberry blond fur. Snacking for a few minutes on morsels of dry food, she sipped some water, flexed her claws and adjourned to her window shelf in my office for a nap. Without missing a beat, Michele's city house and its zany juvenile were behind her forever.

Michele pondered a thought-provoking question concerning feline memory: What would the cut-off time be? Would a three-month, three-day window have erased all thoughts of home?

My computer screen on arriving home (I blame Pat and Gordon).

Fourth Quarter 1996
"How was your trip?"

My *trip*? How was my trip? The usual rundown included a few quick phrases: "Great…the ride of my life…no problems except for that muffler my last day out…drove nearly ten thousand miles…yes, I did take a few pictures, and no, I was never once in fear of my life…"

Will I go back to Texas one day and finish the journey? Not sure where to put that.

What seemed at the time to be highway transitions from one dot on the map to the next, now return as main events—buying groceries in Bridgeport, Nebraska, chatting with *Mrs. Local* about beef tongue, tidy rows of it wrapped in cellophane along with kidney, roasts and hamburger. Why didn't I photograph the rows of beef tongue and kidneys? Instead, I spent a roll of film on Chimney Rock. The world has seen Chimney Rock in a hundred car ads. Next time, one shot of the tourist stop and a few more at the grocery store with fluorescently illuminated organ meats. Next time the goat's head wedged in a square of fencing or the *well-heeled* armadillo crossing the road.

I knew it before I left last May that small towns would be sought, along with a few landmarks along the route like Rushmore and Crazy Horse. Already the remnants push even Rushmore aside. The bar in Hathaway, for one, and Carhenge, boots on fence posts, Sits-With-12741, and the absolute solace of Wounded Knee. The three stooges of Whiteclay, Nebraska, horses at the fence nudging and pushing to remain the star, then tearing off in a wild run to the clouds beyond, turning like synchronized swimmers to charge the fence again, nipping at the rump of another, stopping to stare, gauging my level of interest. *The Madcap Mares* of comic relief to South Dakota's Pine Ridge, a dismal ghetto of idle young men, waiting on the streets at noon—for night.

*****

Epilogue—

College wasn't an option for the likes of me in 1959. My father's sister Arlene, my adopted "single mom" who signed my report cards on the *Guardian* line, was a *cleaning lady* in a classroom building at the University of Rhode Island. It never occurred to me that college was possible, affordable or otherwise. That was for the smart kids. In the business world, girls of means, secretaries of the future—pre-Betty Freidan—*attended* Katharine Gibbs. I got a job after graduation... as a clerk typist.

During school vacations, I would go to work with Arlene, lunch box and all, probably the Roy Rogers version with the cute little thermos. Her *office,* a small coffee room in the basement shared with other janitorial staff, was located in Washburn Hall, a three-story, granite edifice bordering the quadrangle, a word I was curiously proud of knowing. The memory of Washburn Hall is still beguiling, the aroma of the supply room with its forest of pencils, ink bottles, fountain pens, boxes of chalk, bales of legal pads, composition books—black covers flecked with white squiggles, stitched with thread at the inner binding. My favorite classroom with wood floors buffed to a warm shine had giant windows overlooking the quadrangle. Rows of writing chairs faced the large oak desk at the front of the room with an American flag hanging motionless overhead. Recalling it now still conjures the magic of curiosity, of possibilities, although my eight-year-old self hadn't realized it at the time. If Washburn Hall happened to be idle, as in Christmas break, I had the large room all to myself, writing on the board, twirling the revolving chair, teaching my imaginary class from a heavy book, having grasped its content in the same way a dog understands words from a human—they only *appear* to understand; what they hear is *blah blah, supper.* An enormous world map pulled down like a window shade, scrutinized by me for the North Pole and its proximity to Hamilton, Rhode Island. At the age of eight, Santa was real—I had requested a Betsy McCall doll and feared the Jamestown Bridge across Narragansett Bay was too high and might block the way.

Does my youthful exposure to higher education explain the allure of *Classics Illustrated?* There were lots of reasons for spending time at Rudy's Market—comic books like *Little Lulu* and *Tom and Jerry,* not to mention penny candy—but *Classics Illustrated* beckoned. Now we have *This or That for Dummies* and the magic of *Google.* The information never stops. By the way, all of this would have been helpful in 1957 with *A Tale of Two Cities,* fully appreciated in adulthood for its perfect language, but in tenth grade, *OMG!* (Can't recall what our version of *OMG* must have been.)

Have you ever spent time with folks discussing this or that when someone utters a phrase or reference to which everyone but you is hip? Common knowledge apparently, but you're the only one in the room without a clue: a book, movie, artist, or literary reference; everyone is talking about it, and you know nothing. Well, you can look it up now and quick. Again, David Frost and his suggested "art of acquiring new information at random, recalling it hours later with a thick layer of sophistication"—*instant erudition,* I think he called it. While I have not read *Heart of Darkness* in its entirety, for some reason Joseph Conrad whispered to me often. Was Kurtz the imagined troll beneath Brooklyn's Bridge? *That* education!

Whoever cares to learn will always find a teacher.

—German proverb

Vagabond Chic
The Rolling Soundtrack

1. Leave Home – Ted Hawkins – *"Long As I Can See the Light"*
2. The Moose Hunt – Ray Lynch – *"Pastorale"*
3. The Hall in Cooperstown – Carly Simon – *"Take Me Out to the Ballgame"*
4. Sailing Out of Cleveland – Shadows of Knight – *"Gloria"*
5. The Mackinaw Bridge – Enya – *"Exile"*
6. The Greatest Lake – Gordon Lightfoot – *"Wreck of the Edmund Fitzgerald"*
7. Prairie Rose – Peggy Lee – *"Is That All There Is?"*
8. Rushmore – Bruce Hornsby/Bradford Marsalis – *"The Star Spangled B"*
9. Wounded Knee – Bobby McFerrin and Yo Yo Ma – *"Wolf"*
10. The Plains – Dwight Yoakam – *"A Thousand Miles from Nowhere"*
11. Nebraska's Magic Moment – Percy Faith – *"A Summer Place"*
12. Hays, Kansas – Dances with Wheat – *"John Dunbar Theme"*
13. Leave Texas – Bobby Horton – *"Steal Away"*
14. Nod to Graceland – Elvis – *"That's All Right"*
15. Wilfred's Grave – Mike and the Mechanics – *"The Living Years"*
16. Hymn to Him – Jose Feliciano – *"In My Life"*

Joey's Show & Tell
The Stone Collection

Third Connecticut Lake, Pittsburg, New Hampshire
Montgomery, Vermont
Northeast Pennsylvania, I-84
The shore of Lake Erie, Cleveland, Ohio (at
the Rock & Roll Hall of Fame)
The shore of Lake Huron, Mackinac City, Michigan
Superior, Wisconsin (Lots of iron up here)
Moosehead Lake, Moose Lake, Minnesota
Fargo, North Dakota, at the railroad crossing
The Yellowstone River, Forsyth, Montana
The Bighorn Mountains, Sheridan, Wyoming
The base of Crazy Horse Mountain, Black Hills, South Dakota
Wounded Knee Burial Ground, South Dakota
(What happened at Wounded Knee?)
Alliance, Nebraska, at "Car Henge"
Oklahoma City, the site of the bombing
From Leland Calverley, age 11, Wills Point, Texas
Hope Arkansas, McDonald's parking lot
Steele, Missouri (Southeast corner, the tip of the boot heel)
Troy, Tennessee, Highway 51
Central Kentucky, Rte. 64 east
Northeast West Virginia, I-68
Northwest Maryland, I-68
Port Jervis, New York
Connecticut side of the "Welcome to RI" sign, I-95 north

Gloria Jean: *Forties Period Piece*—it quips itself. A Rhode Island native, she was born in tandem with the bombing of Pearl Harbor on December 7, 1941, probably to the tune of Bing Crosby's first public performance of "White Christmas" on NBC radio that year, and named for American actress, child star Gloria Jean.

Following high school graduation, she *attended* the University of Rhode Island as clerical assistant to the Director of Athletics, unique placement for an eighteen-year-old fresh out of school—*total Kismet*—nine years a secretary among football players, phys. ed. majors and a treasured squad of coaches and professors, still mentors to this day: *Yes, Gloria Jean, there's life beyond boys and rock & roll—learn something!* She relished their conversations and even sat in on random classes—Anatomy, Kinesiology—in the company of a life-size skeleton stowed in her office (a tall, lanky locker, his backstage *digs*). Her ongoing college education was prudently gleaned—curiosity is a gift.

Marriage and a move to New Hampshire with her school teacher husband came next. It was 1968 and the remarkable decade to follow—aside from the chaos of headline news—included life with a St. Bernard, the birth of their daughter, and a son three years later. Her continued involvement in creative arts included painting, summer sidewalk shows, photography, publicity writing and set design in community theatre.

It was many years later, inspired by John Steinbeck's *Travels with Charley* and part-time work at a weekly newspaper that served to embolden the vision of her lone journey west. *Vagabond Chic* is her first published work.